THE MONKEY TREE

The MONKEY TREE

Janet S. Anderson

DUTTON CHILDREN'S BOOKS

NEW YORK

Library of Congress Cataloging-in-Publication Data
Anderson, Janet, date.
The monkey tree/by Janet S. Anderson.
p. cm.
Summary: Afraid that she has lost her own artistic ability, fourteen-year-old Susanna feels a connection with her great-uncle Louie, who has spent the past twenty years hidden away in his room, and in trying to reach him, she begins to discover her own inner strength.
ISBN 0-525-46032-2 (hc)
[1. Artists—Fiction.   2. Self-perception—Fiction.   3. Family life—Fiction.
4. Friendship—Fiction.   5. Great-uncles—Fiction.]   I. Title.
PZ7.A5365Mo   1998   [Fic]—dc21   98-24315   CIP   AC

Published in the United States 1998 by Dutton Children's Books,
a division of Penguin Putnam Books for Young Readers
345 Hudson Street, New York, New York 10014
http://www.penguinputnam.com/yreaders/index.htm

DESIGNED BY AMY BERNIKER
Printed in USA
First Edition
2 4 6 8 10 9 7 5 3 1

To John,
with thanks and love

THE MONKEY TREE

Chapter 1

usanna had taught herself how to do them, the things she was scared to do, couldn't do, had to do. The important thing was not to think. What you did instead was concentrate, funnel every bit of energy into looking at what was right in front of you right at this very moment. *Seeing* it. Even lately, when her art had shrunk to a dry little nub deep inside her, she could still do that.

So now, plodding up the stairs, pushing away any thought of what was waiting at the top, she looked. She looked at the stairs, at each gray tread, worn in the middle, corners fat with dust. She looked at the old enameled tray she was carrying, the rose-rimmed sandwich plate wedged between the soup bowl and the teacup, a second plate jammed in the corner, holding the two crumbling brownies dug from the funeral offerings still littering the pantry shelf. This was what he was waiting for up there—this food, this lunch. Her.

It wasn't working. Looking wasn't working, and she'd already reached the half-landing with its window facing her grandparents' side yard. But here at least she could stop, take a deep breath and then another. Try again.

Moving close to the small window, she stared out at the barn, the short gravel driveway, the bit of road just visible from under the trees. On the road somebody was walking, the shape big and somehow familiar. Familiar from the funeral? The whole town had been at her grandmother's funeral. The shape turned, and yes, it was a girl. It was the girl, enormous, black-robed, who'd stood front row center in the choir, crying so hard the tears ran into her open mouth as she sang. Susanna squeezed shut her eyes, waiting for the girl to trundle out of sight. There must be something she could look at that wouldn't remind her of why she was here.

But what else was out there? The swing? All right, then concentrate on the swing. It was interesting from this height, this angle, seeing how the ropes connected with the huge old maple, how different their texture was from the texture of the bark, how they seemed to fall into the leaves and . . . She stood up on tiptoe and peered over the edge of the narrow sill to see how they would reappear. One rope or two? In shade or . . . ?

Tea sloshed onto her hand. Make sure it's hot, her mother had said. Make sure the water boils. Great-uncle Louie can tell, and he won't drink it if it didn't. It was hot. Susanna balanced the tray on a knee and sucked the burn. She really couldn't do this. She shouldn't have to. Now that he was sixteen, Mike could have driven Grandpa to the airport alone. Her mother didn't need to go, especially not at a mealtime, especially when Susanna had never taken a tray to her mother's uncle before, never even been in his room, never even seen him.

Twenty years. How could someone live in one room for twenty years? How would he look? A year ago, Mike's eyes would have lit right up. "Fangs, Suz," he would have said, snarling his best monster snarl. "The guy's sitting there with fangs *this* long." But Mike hadn't teased her for a long time, and the kind of monster that scared her now, at fourteen, was one her older brother wouldn't know anything about. Like crazy. What if the old man waiting up there was . . . crazy?

It *really* wasn't working this time. Susanna shut her eyes and breathed hard in and out, in and out, and then started up the rest of the stairs. Maybe it would help just to count them. Yes. Count them: four, five, six, to the upper landing and the old bureau where she could stop again, rest the tray for a minute, rest. . . .

She liked the upper landing. She liked the wide plank floor, painted gray, with her grandmother's rag rugs lined up over it like dominoes. She liked all the doors, all five of them (six if you counted Uncle Louie's down his little hall), all painted cream, with china knobs. It was a cool space, a little too dim if all the doors were closed, a little dizzy if you leaned out over

5

the railing and stared down, but nice somehow, peaceful, except when Mike was looming at the door of his room, his words unspoken but clear under his silent scowl: "When do we go home? We've got to go home!"

Susanna liked her room, too. It was a tiny room, carved out of the space between the bathroom and the back of the house, a baby's room, really, just big enough for a bed and a small chest of drawers, with a funny little triangle of space where you could hang six things on a pipe behind a flowered curtain. There was a hole in the floor where heat came up from the kitchen.

In the winter. But now it was summer. And her grandmother had just died, her grandmother whom she'd visited only three times that she could remember, because they lived so far away and there was never enough money even when her father had a job, and maybe—she'd never thought of this before—maybe because of Uncle Louie. Her mother had never talked much about Uncle Louie. And all her grandfather had said was that they could have him. *He* was going to Arizona. He'd loved his wife, but now she was gone and he was going to Arizona. They were welcome to the house and everything in it, but Uncle Louie came with it and that was that.

That was that. And *that*, there, waiting, was his room. The hallway to it felt separate from the landing: narrow, bare, echoing. It was darker than the landing, too, with the closed door at the end, and the ceiling . . . she couldn't see the ceiling. Something up there had sucked up what little light there was and swallowed it.

Stop it. Walk. Six, seven, eight, nine steps, balance the tray on your knee, lift up your hand and knock. Do it. Susanna knocked hard twice, as her mother had told her to, turned the smooth china knob, and opened the door.

He was only an old man. He was sitting behind a big round table in the middle of the room, a shadowy old man in the glare from the open French doors behind him. And then Susanna forgot all about Uncle Louie. She set the tray down to get rid of it and began turning, very slowly, as though nudged by a huge gentle hand.

The room was more than beautiful. It was like Aladdin's cave, so rich that Susanna, feeling herself expand trying to take it in, knew she never could, knew that you could never come to the end of beauty like this. There, a tall chest, heavy with drawers. There, a fat desk embellished with brass. There, a row of bookcases jammed with old books, new books, leather-backed and paper-backed, propped up by a whole menagerie of figures: a squat stone bird, a lolling cat, a pink pig smiling down at a grinning puppet sprawled floppy and fantastic in a child's rocker.

A somber ape studied a human skull. A wild-eyed woman stabbed a dragon. And everywhere things hung, draped, jutted, an ordered clutter so immense, so overwhelming, that Susanna literally staggered, grabbing at a tall-backed chair so she wouldn't fall. And then she saw the wall.

It was a wall of pictures, hung ceiling to floor, and Susanna, now almost not breathing, felt the huge hand push her closer and closer and closer. *This* was looking. *This* was

7

seeing. With no thought in her head except to sit, forever, in front of that wall, she turned to reach for the chair behind her.

It was a sound that stopped her, a strangled sound, coming from the table, where the old man had propelled himself up out of shadow to become a tall gaunt figure with a face. But Susanna couldn't see his face, because all she could see were his eyes. And what was there shocked her, shoved her back and out the door and down the hall, his voice echoing and re-echoing behind her even through the slammed door:

"My room! Mine! *Get out!*"

No counting now. Breath rasping, the last few seconds blurred, Susanna found herself down in the living room, huddling deep in her grandfather's huge, cavelike chair. Her heart quieted, finally, slowed by her hand smoothing worn corduroy over and over and over. She was okay. She was okay.

But stunned. She still felt stunned. She had never known a room like that could *be* in an ordinary house, just down a hall from a bathroom, just up some stairs from a kitchen sink. A room like that, blazing, pulsing, *alive.*

But at its center . . . She shivered. Who? What? An old man? Or the kind of monster that haunted her dreams?

And what might happen to her if she tried to find out?

No. Mike was right for once. They couldn't stay here. She couldn't stand any more monsters. No, they should go home, right now, today, as soon as Mike and her mother got back from the airport and her father—

"Susie?" It was as if she'd conjured him, solid, compact, her father, hers, and then she was up and burrowing into him as she hadn't done since she was six years old. He gave a grunt of amusement and hugged her back. "Rough few days, was it? Where's your mom?"

"Airport," she said and stepped back into ordinary life. "Dad, let's go home. Okay? Can we?" Yes, he would say. Now. Soon.

"I don't know," he said. He sank into the desk chair and riffled absentmindedly through the neat stack of brightly colored brochures. "Arizona," he said. "Your grandfather has a perfectly good job teaching high school science, and what does he want to do? He wants to take early retirement and move to Arizona." He shook his head. "How many resumes have I sent out? How many tapes?"

Susanna sagged. She'd heard it so many times. It was all her father could talk about anymore, and she couldn't help it, she was tired of it, tired of it. "You're not a science teacher," she said, feeling she'd said it a hundred times before.

He smiled, sighed. "Yeah, I know. And with all the orchestras folding, there's just a lot of clarinet players out there, aren't there? A lot of *good* clarinet players."

He was a good clarinet player. Susanna had once thought that his web of notes, weaving around her ever since she could remember, would always hold. If he fell through . . .

"But I guess we're not about to starve," he said. "Your mom's job, and of course, all my students . . ."

The web knit back into safety. That part of it at least would never fail. All those students, all those recitals, those wobbly little kids and collapsing music stands and tears. So of course they'd go back.

Why, though? Why did she want to? Once, the answer would have been clear. Once, there would have been so many things to miss. Her room, layered with her life. The park. Her favorite store, "Prints and Books," where, tripping over cats, you sidled down narrow aisles and climbed, sneezing, to drag enormous portfolios from dusty shelves. It still had a center, her town, because of the college, the students, and ever since she was little, perched high on her father's back, Susanna had explored it. She could almost see it now, "their" café, once the Moon Dog, now the Café Caffe, where, at old iron tables, she'd drunk first cocoa, then lemon tea, and finally, wonderfully, just since last winter, a cappuccino so bubbled and frothed it melted like gritty snow on her tongue. All good things, once. But now? She didn't even know if they meant anything anymore.

Because who was there to go with them? Susanna had always had two friends. Who needed more than two friends, she'd always thought. Two friends since always. What she'd never imagined was that Megan might move away. That Amanda might . . . But she'd told herself not to think about Amanda, and what Amanda had done to her. Never, never think about Amanda.

Her father was standing. "I'm going to get cleaned up before your mother gets home. Ten hours each way on a bus for an audition against at least every wind player in the country . . ."

He sighed. "Not anything you ever want to do."

"I'm not a musician," she said, and she meant to hurt him, because she hurt now, all over, and he didn't know, he hadn't noticed, couldn't have done anything to help even if he had. Nothing could help when home was no answer and here, here was the room upstairs and Uncle Louie, and she knew if they stayed she'd have to go up again. She shivered, and then started when her father touched her gently on the arm.

"No," he said, "and thank God for it." His smile was wry. "So you try not to be a musician and I'll try not to drown myself in Grandma's claw-foot tub." He started out the door.

"Daddy?" said Susanna and she hadn't called him that since she was six years old, either. But his words and the image they dragged up were so terrible she could hardly bear to let him go. "You wouldn't really do that, would you?"

He turned, somberly taking in the expression on her face. "It *has* been a rough week, hasn't it? No, babe. I wouldn't really do that. Not ever. And I'm sorry. That was a rotten thing to say. Just let me get cleaned up and I might almost be human again." He tried a smile. "Okay?"

"Okay," said Susanna. But she listened as he made his way up the stairs and across the landing and into the large old bathroom, and it took him a long, long time.

Chapter 2

That's good." Susanna's mother took a long swallow of iced tea and swung her feet up onto the glider. The screened porch was cool this time of day, shaded by lilacs at each corner and by the big maples in the center of the side yard. "I'm not moving from here until suppertime, and then Shirings better still be serving their famous fish fry or we're not eating."

Susanna heard something scrape overhead, and her heart lurched. He was up there, then, outside. They were separated by only a few inches of wood.

"Oh, damn," said her mother. She had heard it, too, and was looking up. "Uncle Louie." She lowered her voice. "Just for a minute, I forgot about Uncle Louie. We could bring him back fish fry, I guess, but then it would be past his usual suppertime. Did he eat much lunch? I didn't see his tray in the kitchen."

Everything was so simple in her mother's world, Susanna thought. You took trays up, you brought them down. Her mother had probably barely noticed what had sent Susanna reeling: the room like the inside of a kaleidoscope, where every movement made a new pattern, each more perfect than the last. Even as she'd turned to run, her eye had snagged on a frieze of laughing children dancing over the small stained-glass window beside the bed. Perfect.

But the tray? "I forgot to get it," she said now, and that was the exact truth. She'd forgotten the tray the second she'd put it down.

"Oh. Well, maybe you'd better. He hasn't been eating much, and I'm trying to keep track. . . ."

Susanna took a deep breath. No. Please, no. "Couldn't Mike?" she said. "It's Mike's turn."

"Mike? I thought I told you; didn't I tell you? Uncle Louie's got this thing about men. He hates them; they scare him. He'd have a fit. The last thing I need right now is Uncle Louie throwing a fit. You don't really mind, do you? Just for tonight. You've been such a help. . . ."

There was no way, then, that Susanna could tell her. She wished she could, wished she could talk to her mother the way some girls seemed able to talk to theirs. But talking had always been hard for her. And to her mother . . . ? It wasn't only that she couldn't see what Susanna saw. It seemed she couldn't listen, either, at least not in the right way.

Right now she wasn't listening at all. She was still talking, thinking out loud, her eyes abstracted. "There's still all those casseroles, aren't there? Mother's church ladies, bless their hearts. Well, she certainly shipped enough casseroles to funerals in her time." Her eyes clouded and filled with tears. "Damn," she said again, swabbing at her face. "I'm sorry. I'll be okay, really I will. It's just, with Grandma gone and Grandpa halfway to Arizona, I'm feeling a bit like an orphan. I'll bet you didn't know people could feel like orphans when they're thirty-nine years old."

Say, do, what? Susanna felt all angles, a Picasso, grotesque. Mike poked his head through the doorway, saw his mother in tears, disappeared. *Hey,* Susanna shouted at him silently. Dad? *Dad?*

But her father wasn't there. "Why's . . . Uncle Louie up there?" she asked, finally, because questions sometimes worked. They distracted. It was even a question she wanted answered. Why *was* he up there? What had led him to go up those stairs and shut that door so long ago?

Her mother took a deep breath and then another long swallow of tea. "Uncle Louie? Yes, you're right, I guess I'm not a complete orphan if I have Uncle Louie. He's Grandma's only brother, you know, but younger, like you and Mike but the other way around. Let's see, then, he must be sixty. Sixty. He seems a lot older than that, doesn't he? And that means he was only about forty when he moved in.

"Good Lord." She was silent a moment, frowning. "Just a year older than I am now. I can hardly believe it. I thought he was ancient. Not that I saw much of him. I was in college then, but when I came home my first Christmas, there he was, up in that room just like he is now. I did a few things for him, for your grandma, really: took his laundry up, that kind of thing. He always thanked me, made a little joke. He could be funny, Uncle Louie. And once he even gave me a present, that little picture of Grandma I've got in my bedroom at home."

"Did you ever talk to him?"

"Talk to him? Like a real person, you mean? Like an uncle?" Her mother thought for a minute and shrugged her shoulders. "No. Maybe we were both too shy. He talked to your grandmother, though. I'd hear them sometimes in there, laughing. It wasn't until later I realized that Grandpa must have heard them too. Laughing. Leaving him out."

She sighed. "Poor Grandpa. I mean, if you think about it, he never really had Grandma to himself. Before Uncle Louie, you know, Grandma's father lived here. He'd given her this house when she married, and moved to a smaller place, but after a while he got crippled with arthritis and moved back in. Your grandmother, of course, could never say no to somebody who needed her. Especially not her own father.

"But oh, boy, Grandpa Grinell. He was something else, your great-grandpa was. At least Louie stays up there quietly and doesn't bother anybody, but Grandpa Grinell . . . I know now he was probably in awful pain, but at the time I just figured he liked being miserable. He certainly made my life miserable all through my teens, I can tell you that.

"Anyway, he died, starting with the hip he broke falling on

the cellar stairs where he had no business being. He could hardly *walk*. So he fell, and then he yelled and yelled all the time the Rescue was carrying him out of the house and up the driveway." She shivered and set down her glass. "I'll never forget that, how he sounded and the look on my mother's face. . . ."

The look on her mother's face. It curled Susanna up into a ball, twisted her away as far as she could get. What could she say; there was nothing she could say. But then her eyes caught on her father coming through the door. He stared at her, puzzled. Your mother's upset, his face said. Why aren't you comforting your mother? He circled around her and sat down next to his wife.

"Hey, Meggie," he said. "You okay?"

"Yeah," she said. "Yeah," and then settled hard against him and let out a deep breath. "I'm glad you're home."

"It's not." Mike, outside, was a soft blur behind old screens, but his voice was jagged. "It's not home. So what's the deal? Now you're back, Dad, can we go?"

No, Susanna thought. Not again. Not now. She slid out of her chair and was almost off the porch before her father stopped her. "Hey. Both of you. A problem and you complain? You run? What is this?"

"Mom asked me," Susanna said. The door was stained, peeling, a leaf from a hundred years ago stuck to the bottom. "To find something, some dinner for Uncle Louie. Okay?"

"Maybe not," he started, but his wife gave his hand a squeeze.

"It's all right, Jack," she said. "I know you're tired. But they're tired, too. Susanna's been helping me clean and then she had to get lunch for Uncle Louie. And you should have seen the traffic once we got near the airport. I was glad it wasn't me driving. Mike did a terrific job. No, you run along, Susanna. And, Mike, come tell your dad about those yearbooks Grandpa dug up, how funny the football uniforms were back then. Mike didn't know his grandpa was star quarterback his senior year. . . ."

Susanna escaped. She *was* tired. But she'd been tired all spring, ever since those two terrible days, a month apart, that had somehow reduced everything she had thought she was to rubble. First Amanda, and then Mrs. Albright. "This is no good, Susanna," Mrs. Albright had said, handing back Susanna's final project with a grade Susanna had never seen on her art because she'd only ever seen A's. "There's nothing interesting here. Nothing new. In fact, I can't believe you put any work into this at all. I'm disappointed in you. I'm very disappointed."

Isn't that what Amanda had said, just in different words? But she wasn't letting herself think about Amanda, remember? It was just so hard, not thinking. Amanda was so much a part of her, or of who she used to be.

She and Amanda and Megan. Her mother had called them the Bermuda Triangle, because she said when the three of them were there, the whole house got sucked into Susanna's room and disappeared. "No," she would pretend to moan.

"Not my last pair of scissors. Not the whole roll of paper. No!" But she hadn't really minded, had fueled them happily with crackers and juice, and extravagantly admired all the projects and paintings and puppet shows that for years had flowed out in a steady stream.

For years and years and years. Tall, lanky Amanda with her frizz of red hair, rolling all over the floor of Susanna's room, trying to tell the joke she'd heard at recess but laughing too hard to get it out. Tiny Megan, her face scrunched in concentration, showing them the new step she'd learned in ballet and falling, shrieking, into a tangle of feet. And Susanna, average size, average everything she would have said, but who effortlessly, it seemed, overflowed with what Megan called "the good stuff."

"We need something *new*," she'd say, dancing into the room. "Come on, Susanna. The good stuff, we need some of the good stuff." And something wonderful always seemed to be there, waiting to pop out of Susanna's brain.

Used to be. Not anymore. And now she could hear her brother, his words clear even through the closed porch door. "Football," he was saying. "Varsity starter. Kim. *Home.*" And then, even louder, clearer, the sentence whole: "Of course she doesn't care. She doesn't *have* any friends."

The living room rug was scratchy under her bare feet, the step into the kitchen a relief, old linoleum, worn and smooth. From the pantry came the gentle groan of the freezer, squeezed hard by cupboards. Susanna sank into her grandmother's rocker. It squeaked. Ragged cookbooks flanked one side, the cellar door the other. They'd always been there. They'd been there forever.

Everything else had changed. Not just Amanda. Not just her art. Mike had been proud of her once, his strange little sister who could draw. But not now. Not lately. Lately, he just avoided her. He seemed embarrassed to have her around. And her parents, once comfortable shadows, now kept looming up, bumping into her. They expected . . . She rocked again, again, back and forth, back and forth. Expected what? Back and forth, but now it was her head, because she didn't know. She didn't know.

She remembered one of the times she'd been here—she must have been six or seven. Her grandmother had worn an apron, pink, with flowers, clean, but stained; her heart was a soft steady thump against Susanna's face pressing into pink blur. They had just arrived. And when, finally released, Susanna had looked up, she hadn't understood. Crying? Why was her grandmother crying?

"Because you're here, sweetie. I'm so happy you're here."

She was still here, but it wasn't enough.

"Hey." It was her brother, slouching uneasily in the doorway.

"What?"

"They want you. He wants you, up there."

"Where?" Stupid. She knew. She knew.

"Up there." He shifted, not meeting her eyes. "Can't you hear him? He's been pounding for ten minutes."

Susanna curled up, hugging her knees. It was all she seemed able to do anymore.

"You go," she said.

"I *can't*. You know what Mom said. He hates guys. He'd throw a fit if I went."

"Susanna?" The word came from far away, from the porch, but it was enough to uncurl her, pull her up with its power. "Susanna?" her mother called again. "Please?"

Susanna pushed by her brother and started up the stairs.

Chapter 3

A mass of something slumped in the shadows at the
end of the hall. It looked dead, and then she made
a lurch away that shaped it, named it. It was the tray, Uncle
Louie's tray from lunch. She took a step toward it, and the
pounding stopped. Okay, I'm coming. But I'm not going in. Not.

But when she crouched down to pick up the tray, she knew
she might have to. The food was untouched, a piece of paper
splayed across the bowl of soup. The soup, tomato, had
soaked through it so that the word written there was blurred.
But the large black letters were clear enough. MARY, they
read.

Susanna backed down the hall and propped the shaking tray
on the landing railing. *Mary*. Mary was her grandmother, and

she was dead. She had died of a heart attack a week ago. Uncle Louie must know. He *did* know. Susanna's grandfather had told him, and when they'd arrived, he'd told them Uncle Louie's response. "He nodded," her grandfather had said, his voice shaking. "I told him his sister had died, the sister who'd taken care of him for twenty years. . . . He nodded."

The pounding started again. Think. Find a way. But not down. Down was Mike's "no," her mother's "please," her father's puzzled eyes. Her room? Her bed, with pillows to jam over her ears and shut it out, shut everything out? But they wouldn't let her shut it out.

She slid the tray onto the scaly dark bureau that had stood on the landing forever and stared into the mirror. It was splotchy with age: in it she was old, too, an old fourteen-year-old with heavy eyebrows and heavy, skinned-back hair. She backed away, turned, ran down the hall, and swung open Uncle Louie's door. She shut it, leaned against it, and then stared fixedly at the old man staring back at her from behind his table. She took a deep breath and said it. "She's dead. Mary's dead."

Uncle Louie slowly nodded. He pushed aside the pad and the marker from in front of him and, with a trembling hand, touched his chest. "*She* died, too, remember? Mother? She died, too."

"Your mother? She died of a heart attack, too?" said Susanna. She tried to puzzle it out. "Is that why you weren't surprised when Grandpa told you? Then why did you write that? Write *Mary*? If you knew?"

22

"I thought . . . maybe . . ." His puzzled eyes studied her one more moment, and then he covered them with a shaking hand. When he opened them again, he seemed surprised to still see her. "Who are you?" he said.

Susanna looked down at the floor and immediately forgot anything else. Where had he found a rug like that? It glowed, no, it pulsed with color, with every color, with all colors, with the sun and the heat of very far away, very long ago. Its pattern dizzied her, and she found herself suddenly on her knees, tracing the melding of one perfect geometry into another, and then memory flooded over her.

She remembered crawling, crawling; she'd crawled by choice long after she'd learned how to walk. People had laughed at her, nagged her, but what was walking compared with the ever-changing universe under your knees, under your hands and eyes? She could still see them, feel them: wood floors with their cracks and tiny nails, linoleum lumpy with flowers, bright scatter rugs of soft cotton tufts, bristling brown doormats. Living rooms were endless, every rug different: smooth, shaggy, whorled, scratchy. . . .

Happy. That's what was engulfing her now, that old happiness of total immersion in texture, color, pattern, the beauty of it, the *sense* of it. She looked up, wanting something she hadn't dared want for months, to express it, that joy, to share it.

Uncle Louie was staring fixedly at her again, his head forward like an old turtle. His eyes were focused now, and urgent. "Twenty-five years ago I bought it," he said. "A little hole of a store in New York, but they knew what they were selling. I paid a ransom for it, much more than I could afford. But not enough. Nobody could pay what it's worth, could they? Because you can't really own something like that, can you? Except . . ." and his hand fluttered to his chest again. "Except in here."

Susanna nodded. "It's the most beautiful thing I've ever seen," she said. Then she sat back on her heels and lifted her hands to the whole room. "It's all . . . the most beautiful thing I've ever seen."

His face blazed suddenly with joy. "It is, isn't it? You see that, don't you?" He leaned up out of his chair, reaching toward her and then, just as suddenly, the light dimmed back into confusion. "Who *are* you?" he asked again.

Susanna stood up. She wasn't sure how she felt, but she knew she was no longer afraid. "I'm her granddaughter. Mary's granddaughter." And then she remembered something else, a real gift she could give in exchange. "I was named after her," she said. "At least my middle name. Mary."

"Mary," he said, and this time he did touch her, his fingers gentle on her hand. "Yes," he said, and sank slowly back, nodding. He sat, still nodding, his gaze now inward. Then he began to scowl and he straightened again, his neck rigid.

"I paid my way," he said fiercely. "Every month, I wrote my check." He slapped the table. "But not to *him*. *He's* not getting any of it."

"Who?" said Susanna. "Grandpa?" What was it her

mother had said? That he hated men? But her grandfather? Her small, gentle grandfather? "Grandpa?" she repeated.

But Uncle Louie sagged just as suddenly back, his anger spent. He looked up at Susanna now with the most desolate eyes she'd ever seen. "She's really gone, isn't she?" he said. "Really gone." And then a tear trickled very slowly up over the rim of his eye and down his cheek.

Without thinking, Susanna took two steps toward him. No, he didn't scare her anymore. The only fear left in her now was her usual fear of not knowing what to do or say. And what *could* she do? It was her grandmother he wanted, not her. Okay, then. What would her grandmother have done to comfort her little brother Louie?

And then she saw her again, her grandmother in her flowered pink apron in the middle of the kitchen. Susanna reached over and touched the old man's sleeve. "Yes," she said. "She's gone. But I think she left something for you. So wait, okay? Wait."

Downstairs in the pantry, the freezer wooshed softly open. In front were Corningware, Pyrex, other people's casseroles, scrawled with labels of other people's cooking, other people's ownership. She pushed them aside. There were things behind them, things that she'd seen days ago, hunting for ice cream, but hadn't recognized for what they were. She bent down, gripping the door handle, cold air streaming down her front and her legs, curling her toes. She reached in.

Her grandmother had never had a microwave. The meals

she'd made for her brother Louie to eat after her death were packed in TV dinner trays, old aluminum ones, divided. MEAT LOAF, one read, in neat capitals. MASHED AND GRAVY. CANDIED CARROTS. ONE HOUR AT 350°. On the next shelf were desserts, rows of plastic margarine containers, some new looking, others dim and scratched. APPLESAUCE. PEACH COBBLER. BROWN BETTY. They were all there.

Which? She closed her eyes, confident that her hands would choose right. POT ROAST, she read, pulling it out. Fumbling one shelf down, she grabbed again. CHOCOLATE CAKE. Good. She shut the freezer door.

But the oven stopped her. It was gas. She had a dim memory of her grandmother crouching, doing something inside with a long match. Yes, the blue tin, shelved over the burners, was still there, still full of matches. But what did you do with them? Trying to remember, she pulled open the oven door. Inside, it was black with age, burned rust flaking down. The small hole stared up at her.

With difficulty, she yanked out the heavy old rack, centered the battered tray, shoved. Okay, pot roast in. But the matches . . . One broke at the head. The second flared, yes, but reaching down with it, her hand bumped a knob. The match dropped, glowed sullenly against the scarred linoleum, died. *Be careful!* She struck a third. It burned brightly, and she angled it carefully in, tensing for what she remembered. *Poof*, it would go. *Poof.* It didn't.

"You have to turn on the gas."

Susanna started. But her father was smiling; he was crouching next to her, smiling. "See? Here. You light another match and I'll . . ." They fumbled companionably for a moment and then, when the gas lighted with a satisfying pop, they both sighed. "What temperature do you want?"

"Three-fifty," she said, and watched carefully as he turned up the knob.

"One of the few things I can do," he said. "My parents had one of these, too, and when I wasn't practicing I was heavily into peanut butter cookies."

"Just a little burned," said Susanna, hoarse, hoping, and he laughed.

"Yeah," he said. "You got that one from me. That for Uncle Louie?"

She nodded. He touched her shoulder lightly and then stood up. "Well, when you get him squared away, we're going to head up to Shirings and some supper."

"Do we have to wait?" Mike came, as always, out of nowhere, his huge frame blocking the door. "I'm starved."

"I'm not," said Susanna. Except, maybe, to be left alone, because too much had happened that afternoon, too many people, too many emotions. "I'm really not. And this'll be at least an hour. Can I just stay here?"

"Well, I suppose we could bring you back something," said her father. "I'm pretty hungry myself, actually. Are you sure?"

She nodded. He started for the living room, stopped. "Who's that?" he said. "On the back steps?"

On the back steps was a girl. It was the girl Susanna had seen earlier, but now, closer, she was bigger, she was enormous, and she was jiggling, a rhythmic jiggling to unheard music. As they watched, she shook herself down, pursed her lips, and began knocking on the back door.

Chapter
4

It looks like you have a visitor," said Susanna's father. "We'll see you later, then. Fish fry okay or would you rather have a hamburger?"

Susanna froze. "What do you mean, me? I don't know her."

Mike shot a half-glance at her, a half-grin. "Sure you do. She was in the choir at the church last week, how could you miss her? Turns out she lives in that dump of a place up the road. She grabbed me yesterday when I was coming back with the mail and asked me if I wanted to go to her church youth group Saturday night. I mean, they're going bowling, right?" He grimaced. "But I thought," he glanced again at Susanna, "well, she's not much older than you, so I thought maybe, you know, you might . . ." He looked away, took a breath, went on. "So I said, hey, I can't, not me, but I got this little sister. . . ." He threw up his hands defensively at the look on Susanna's face. "So, I'm sorry. I was just trying to . . ."

Why had he picked now to start acting again like a brother, a brother she wanted to hug and throttle at the same time? But this was no time to think about it. The knocking continued, and only her father could save her. "Dad? You go, please? Please?" It was no good.

"You can say no, you know," he said. He was shaking his head at Mike, but his mouth was twitching. "Bowling," he said, and then they were both gone.

Sick. She was going to be sick. No. She'd say it now. *No. Go away. Go away.*

She opened her eyes and the girl was going. Slowly, slowly she was going, hardly able to carry the weight put on while she'd knocked and no one had come. Her head was sunk between hunched shoulders, her hand coming up to swipe her face. Oh, God, was she crying? Susanna stumbled, righted herself, and wrenched open the back door. The knob slid, sweaty, but held her up. Just.

"Hi," she said.

The girl stopped, swayed on the last step.

Susanna coughed, almost choked, then got it out. "Sorry it took so long," she said. "I, uh, my brother . . ."

"I'll bet he didn't tell you, did he?" said the girl, turning slowly. "About the bowling. If he's like my brother, he probably doesn't tell you anything at all." She peered up at Susanna. "You don't look much like him, do you?"

She didn't look like anybody, hardly human, a blob. Her fat, where it wasn't held down by clothes, bulged; her hair was short, too short, mean. Susanna stepped back and then stopped. She can't hurt you, how can she hurt you? Besides, *you* opened the door. So be polite. Look at her. Look.

The girl's eyes were a surprise, big and brown, puppylike, but no, not puppylike. Her eyes were shrewd and wary, as though nothing much escaped them, and a lot of it hurt.

"Do you?" repeated the girl. "Can I come in?"

Susanna wordlessly opened the door farther and backed away. The girl labored up the stairs, stopped at the top to catch her breath. She looked appraisingly at Susanna and then nodded. "But you look like *her*," she said. "Your grandmother, right? Mrs. Grahame was your grandmother, wasn't she? She wore her hair like that, and your eyebrows are the same." Still nodding, she squeezed by Susanna into the kitchen and lowered herself into the rocker.

"I loved that woman. You probably saw me at the funeral. I was crying so hard I could hardly sing. I used to come over here a lot, and the last time I was here, before she died, she was making those cookies, you know those ones she made that always tasted different from the last time because she never measured anything? And she always let me eat as many as I wanted. She never counted. She liked me to be here, she said, she *liked* me." The girl rocked back hard, her face working.

Then she sighed and sighed again. "So anyway, she was making her cookies and she had her music going . . ."

Susanna had found a chair, sat. She felt dazed by the wash of words, hypnotized, but not in a bad way. She wanted to hear more. But why? The day had been weird enough already, hadn't it, so why did she want this girl to keep talking? Because she was talking about Susanna's grandmother, that was why. Because Susanna had never really known who her grandmother was.

"Yeah, there's her tape player on the fridge, all her tapes. You never knew what you were going to hear. It was like the cookies; it was always different. But that time, that last time, it was Bruce Springsteen, the *Born in the U.S.A.* tape, you know, and she was singing along with it. It was so loud she didn't even hear me knock at first." She leaned forward in the rocker, her head nodding, her body unmoving. "'No retreat, baby, no surrender,'" not singing, but a chant, rhythmic. "'No retreat, baby, no surrender.'" She closed her eyes and rocked back again hard, once, and stopped.

Cookies, okay, they went with the pink flowered apron. But her grandmother and . . . "Springsteen?" Susanna's voice was hoarse. "Are you sure?"

"My name's Melody," said the girl, her eyes still closed. "That's a laugh, isn't it?" She really seemed to expect an answer this time. At least her mouth was shut firmly. Your turn.

Her turn. "My dad," Susanna began finally, but she was still hoarse. She cleared her throat. "He's a musician? He'd say there were lots of different kinds of melodies."

The girl wasn't buying it. "What would *you* say?"

Trapped. What would *she* say? Why was the kitchen so hot? Oh, yeah, the oven. There was just the faintest smell of pot roast. It still needed forty-five minutes, no escape there. What to say? Susanna took a deep breath and gave, not an answer, maybe, but for some reason the truth. "I'd say everybody thinks I'm weird. Especially my brother. And you're right. He didn't tell me about the bowling, until just now. But . . ." But? It had been a long time since she'd been around somebody who hurt worse than she did. So she closed her own eyes and said it. "But it sounds like it might be kind of fun."

Bowling? She didn't know how to bowl. What was she saying?

They both opened their eyes at the same time and stared at each other for a long moment. Then Melody nodded. "It is," she said. "Of course, you'll have to put up with some praying, and Reverend McGill wears these really awful pants. They kind of come up to his chin; they're pathetic. And when he gets a strike he whinnies, but he hardly ever gets a strike."

Doomed, Susanna thought. She was doomed. But what else could she do? She nodded.

Melody heaved herself out of the rocker. "The lanes are good, though. They're really old with all these old signs and calendars, but they keep them up. And they make these really good french fries and milkshakes." Her smile was twisted now, her eyes hard. "And I know what you're thinking, but I don't care, nobody keeps me from my french fries. And you

33

know what? I'm the best bowler there. We meet at the church tomorrow at seven, okay?"

No, thought Susanna. Please, no. But she nodded again. Doomed.

Melody was staring at a spot by the stove. "Really? You'll really come?" Her eyes filled, suddenly, with tears. "She used to stand there, your grandmother, turning chicken, mostly. I remember chicken. But one time I stayed overnight because my dad—well, never mind about my dad—but I, we, stayed over, and in the morning she made this stuff? You had to keep stirring it? Most of her cooking was great, but this stuff, well, it kind of tasted like glue. Of course, we ate it anyway. Some things you didn't complain about with her, you know. She could get tough about some things. She was a tough lady." Melody snuffled hard and scrubbed an arm over her face. "Oh, man," she said. "Oh, man, I miss her."

"Cream of Wheat." It had just come blurting out, the words out of nowhere, the memory . . . And the memory was a gift, a gift she needed because she'd hardly known her grandmother. At the funeral, she'd cried only because of the strangeness, the ugliness of the little church, and her mother's choked sobs. But here was a second memory, strong and alive, to hug to herself. Cream of Wheat . . . Yes, she could remember it so clearly now. Her grandmother stirring, the brown sugar and cream, her grandmother smiling. "So happy because you're here," she'd said. Susanna's own eyes filled with tears now, and she knew that her grandmother would have smiled again at what she was going to say.

"I'll come," she said. "Bowling. I'll come. Do I have to wear anything special?"

"Oh, we're not that religious," Melody said, slowly blinking herself back into the present. Then she shook herself down like she'd done earlier, and when she spoke again her voice was brisk, under control. "But it's two dollars a game, so bring some money. And if your brother changes his mind, bring him, too. Tell him all the girls that come don't look like us." She was gone.

Like us? Susanna felt like she'd been punched in the gut, punched back into the reality of who she was. Like us, Melody had said. Susanna dug her fingers into her ribs, shaking her head. No, she wasn't fat, but that wasn't what Melody had meant. She'd meant what Amanda now thought. Everybody probably. That Susanna was grotesque. Ugly *like* the fat, not human, really, not normal. Not normal.

Something was buzzing, buzzing until she finally turned it off. The pot roast was done.

Chapter 5

He didn't eat it?" Susanna's toast dropped from her fingers and fell, jam side down, onto the floor. She scrabbled for it and then threw it, hard, into the sink. Right. So yesterday hadn't accomplished anything at all.

"No, he didn't," said her mother. "And he didn't want any breakfast this morning, either, except for some tea. I'm not sure what to do. He says he's not sick—at least he didn't say anything when I asked him if he was."

Mike's spoon clattered, his eyes hopeful. "Maybe he *is* sick. Maybe . . ."

"Slide any farther down that hole, Mike, and you'll never crawl out." His father poured more coffee into his mug and watched the steam. "#1 Teacher," the mug read, an old mug with a crack, her grandfather's. The sun was hot on Susanna's back, the granola too sweet, all the store had. He didn't eat it, the food she'd found for him. And she'd told him Mary had made this. Mary.

She felt her father's eyes. "Practice," he said, and whistled a quick perfect scale. The high C hung, then disappeared like music always did. Like all sound did. Like everything. "He didn't eat it, but you made it. Think of it as practice."

"Look," said Mike. They all looked. Blond hair, square perfect face, square perfect everything. Susanna remembered last fall, his last game, the mud mixing with snow, Mike, an anonymous giant in a giant herd, but their giant. Their eyes had never left him. That was where *he* belonged, he was right about that, he knew. So lucky, Susanna thought, swamped suddenly with longing. Would she ever know it again, that solid, safe, certain sense of who she was, where she belonged? Mike was so lucky.

"Look," he said again. "I just don't get it. We come here for Grandma . . . Grandma's . . . and then Grandpa just takes off. I mean, why do we have to deal with . . . I never even met the guy. And I mean, there's four of us, we've got lives, you know, not just me. Mom's job. Dad, sure, so the orchestra's folded, but what about all those kids you teach, that one you're always talking about, he's so good?"

"Mike, we don't know." His mother hunched forward, blue bathrobe flapping, bare toes curled around the rung of her chair. "Don't you see? That's the point. It's a mess. We know you don't want to stay here, but there's other things, not just Uncle Louie."

"Like what?"

"Like I don't have a job," said his father. "And the chances of my getting one in music back home are pretty well zilch. Like we could live here free. Like we've heard they're desperate for special-ed teachers in the rural schools, so your mother could—"

"Yeah, that's probably all they use in this place."

His father ignored him. "And there's even a pretty good chance of finding students here." He shrugged. "Well, that's premature. And Susanna . . ."

He hesitated. The refrigerator clicked on loudly, and outside the window two squirrels corkscrewed up a tree. Susanna what? she thought. Everyone stayed silent, carefully not looking at her, Susanna, the freak. So polite they were. So embarrassed. We've got lives, he'd said, but her? He didn't say her. The tree was suddenly blurred, impressionistic, the world through water. Susanna blinked back her tears.

"Susanna would be changing schools anyway," he continued. "And you'd finally be in the same building, with the same schedule. You could help each other out."

"Oh, great," said Mike. "Oh, sure."

"Stop it, Mike." His father's voice was sharp, finally, impatient.

"Susanna?" said her mother. "How do you feel? If we

stayed the summer, maybe longer, we don't know, we just don't. . . . But your art?"

Susanna wished she could shout it like Uncle Louie. *My room! Mine! Get out!* Then she felt eyes again, but this time they were Mike's. Please, help me, Suz, they were saying. I've got to get *home*! Why did he feel he could slam her one minute and ask for help the next? Well, he couldn't. She met his gaze calmly and shrugged. "I don't care," she said.

Her father sighed, then shook his head at them both. "Of course you care," he said. "But I'm sure we could track down a teacher for you here, if the school didn't come through with somebody good. Anyway, your art's *you*. It's in your bones. You'd do it on the moon if you had to. Like me. My music. Which I'd better go practice." But he sat, swirled a last inch of coffee, swallowed.

Susanna stared at him. What was he saying? "Your art's you"? as though that was the most obvious fact in the world. As though nothing had changed?

But now he was talking to Mike. "Give us these two weeks to sort things out, Mike," he was saying. "That won't kill you, two weeks here until your grandfather gets back from checking out Arizona and makes his plans. He was serious about the garage, by the way, he wants it painted. He'll pay. Keep in shape, make a little money. Training doesn't start until August, does it? Let it rest, okay, give it a rest. Believe me, there's no chance we'll make plans for the fall without consulting you. Besides—"

"You can say no, you know." Mike jerked his head toward Susanna. "That's what you told her. You can say no, you said. So I can too, right? I can always—"

His father stood abruptly. "The scrapers, painting stuff are in the garage. I'm going to practice. Susanna, speaking of no, whatever happened about bowling?"

Susanna resurfaced, Mike's voice echoing in her head. You can say no, he'd said. Sure you can. You can say no, people tell you, but they never tell you *how* to say it. It was like smiling. Smile, people say, and you're just supposed to know how. Just do it. It was supposed to be so easy. Except that it wasn't. Ever. "I'm going," she said, because there was no other answer.

"Good. Maybe you'll meet . . . whoever. Good." He and Mike disappeared out opposite doors, and the kitchen settled into silence.

Her mother was staring at her juice glass, lost in thought. Susanna slowly uncoiled as the kitchen slowly brightened. Space and silence cleared things just as they always had, cleared the air. They let you see and breathe. The counter sat bathed in light, the toaster, the jelly jar gathering it, changing it, handing it back. Colors vibrated, the yellow of the magazines on the refrigerator harsh against the soft butter of the sugar bowl.

This, this was hers. Susanna's. Her father was right about that, at least. This hadn't changed, what she could see, how it made her feel. But if she could never use it again, make it her own on paper or canvas because she wasn't good enough, would never be good enough. . . . A sudden pain caused her to look down and she saw that her hands were clenched so tightly that her nails were digging into her palms.

"I used to go bowling," said her mother. "It's probably the same place, Pokey's, down in Nelson. Who's this girl Dad said came over?"

Susanna crashed back. This girl Dad said came over? "Melody," she said.

"I don't think I know her. Your dad said she lived down the road. I wonder if it's the old Harding place. I hope not. Whoever bought it turned it into a real slum. Mrs. Harding must be spinning in her grave. She had the most beautiful flowers, beds of daffodils in the spring, and she'd trained roses up the side of the shed. The shed burned last fall, Grandma wrote me, and they haven't cleared the wreck away yet. And the yard . . . Did you see that, they have all that junk in the front yard and weeds a foot high? People move from the city, they think 'the country,' but there's country and country. This is a village, not God's Little Acre."

"I don't know," said Susanna. Melody, bowling tonight, maybe if she shoved them away hard enough they'd keep moving, spin out of sight, disappear. Talk about something else, something that maybe her mother could actually do something about. Like Uncle Louie. "Mom, why isn't Uncle Louie eating?"

"He's grieving. I think your grandpa was wrong about that. I think Louie knows more than anyone what he's lost. Lost. That's how he feels now, I think. Like he doesn't

41

know what to do now, or who he is. Does that make any sense?"

Oh, yeah, thought Susanna, and just thinking that made her realize how much she wanted him to be okay. "Will he . . . get better?" she asked her mother now.

"I don't know. Talking would help him, but he won't talk, at least he won't talk to me; story of my life." She touched Susanna briefly. "And if he doesn't start eating . . . You asked me yesterday why he came here, and I don't think I answered. Your grandmother and he were always very close, but especially as kids. I got the impression that she felt she was responsible for him, responsible for protecting him, because he was one of those people born without a skin, she said, you know, hypersensitive so that everything hurt him or upset him or sent him into a rage."

"Scared him."

"That's right," said her mother. "Scared him." She glanced at Susanna. "Like all of us get scared from time to time, isn't that right? Because life isn't always as easy as we'd like it to be?"

Susanna nodded but kept her eyes carefully on the floor. Her mother waited another minute, then sighed and went on. "Scared him. And he was an artistic kid—maybe that's where you got it from—and his father, Grandpa Grinell, remember, well, he *hated* that, thought it was sissy, you know, unmasculine, kept trying to ridicule him out of it, wouldn't let him take lessons, all that kind of thing. Pushed him toward science, math. And, actually, Uncle Louie was good at math, good enough to do really well, eventually, in the stock market. He made quite a lot of money, I take it. Enough, anyway."

Artistic. Of course. Nobody could create a room like that without an artist's brain, eye, hand. She had seen that, and he had seen that she had. "Maybe that's where you got it from," her mother had just said. What if . . .

"Susanna, are you even *listening*?"

Susanna resurfaced. "Oh, yeah, yeah, I am. 'Enough,' you said. Enough for what?"

"Enough to start doing the art he *said* he'd always wanted to do, where he'd always wanted to do it. In his old house with the one person he'd always loved. Where he could feel safe, now that his father was safely dead." She stopped and stood abruptly, slopping the rest of her coffee. "I'd better get dressed."

Susanna moved over to the rocker and slowly began to rock. Uncle Louie was an artist. Yes. Of course. But then why hadn't she seen any easel, brushes, paints? She certainly hadn't smelled that smell that seeped into everything when you were working, the smell of colors and solvents, charcoal and paper. The smell she loved more than anything else in the whole world, and that she'd slammed the door on when she'd left the art room in June, slamming away, too, the sound of her teacher's words. You're not working, Susanna. You're not trying. You're no good.

Had that happened to Uncle Louie, too? But how could it? In his safe room, with the sister he loved, there'd been no one to hurt him. No one to criticize, to make judgments, to tell him

43

he'd failed. No, if his work had stopped, it was because . . .

Well, because she was gone, of course. Mary was gone, and nothing anymore felt safe to him at all. And why create when there was no one left to see?

What if . . . She remembered again the one second yesterday when his face had opened into joy. She'd done that.

What if she could do it again?

Chapter 6

It was still hot at six forty-five, and the paved road outside her grandfather's front door sucked gently at Susanna's shoes before she moved to the gravel of the shoulder. She couldn't believe she was really doing this, had *agreed* to do it. Melody, bowling, all day she'd squashed them out of sight, her mind churning instead with the old man upstairs, who he might be and what he might mean. But an hour ago, her mother had handed her a five-dollar bill, and she'd discovered the evening ahead wasn't squashed at all but was now a huge lump wedged right at the bottom of her throat.

Maybe she could get lost. But you couldn't get lost here. This town wasn't even a town but just two crossed roads, with the church only a little way past the post office, where you had to go every day to pick up your mail. In two minutes she'd see it, the church's square cupola, scraped down; somebody was painting it.

Why was there only one word for it, painting? The same word for cupolas and canvas? It was like "playing." Playing in an orchestra, she'd thought, going to her first concert, four years old. She'd been so excited, thinking she'd be watching her father play—with what? Balls? Sand? A giant board with giant pieces? She'd never even thought of music. Music was what her father did for hours every day in his downstairs room at home. Music was her father's *work*.

A car lumbered past her now, then a pickup, a second car. Where were they all going? Shirings? "The mall," Mike called it, in quotation marks, sarcastic. But he was right, really, because when you rattled open the door into the shabby building, everything was there: groceries, housewares, a Laundromat, a restaurant. There was even a bar around back, another entrance.

Yes, they were all turning left at the crossroads, but she wouldn't. She'd go right when she got there, then across the main road, then down. Or up? Which was which? No hill, so how did you know? She didn't.

This wasn't working any better than it had yesterday, her attempt to take her mind off what lay ahead. The lump was growing now, down into her stomach. Great, first she couldn't breathe, now she was probably going to be sick. She gulped down air, forcing herself to concentrate on the house she was passing now. It was smaller than her grandfather's, yes, but whoever lived there had a good eye. They'd painted it a soft green, just right against the brighter grass, the darker leaves. And then they'd painted the shutters a soft mud. It looked good. It worked.

But the next house. The next house . . . The bushes the neighbors had planted to hide it didn't stand a chance. Eyesore was a good word: looking at the next house just plain hurt. Melody's house? Well, Mike had called it a dump, and that's what it looked like, the yard littered with appliances, plumbing parts, a broken bike. And there was the burned shed her mother had mentioned, blackened, barely standing. Except . . . Susanna stopped, peered, trying to see. It was green, growing, a tendril of something climbing . . . A rose.

"Hey! Hey? Wait up!" The voice caught her, and turning she saw Melody's vast shape silhouetted behind the torn screen of a door. "April, if you're coming, come." The door banged once, and then again. Susanna froze. Two of them? There were two of them she'd have to talk to? And they were just the start. She was crazy to do this, crazy.

But Melody, catching her breath, took care of talking, rattling off a barrage of questions and barely waiting for Susanna's replies. "I didn't get your name. Susanna? Yeah, well this is April, my sister. I didn't really think you'd get your brother out but it was worth a try. He's really a hunk, you know, but guys like that always have girlfriends already, right? Kim? Is that her name? A cheerleader, right? Sure. That figures. But you came, anyway." For somebody so big she could move, and Susanna found herself half running to keep up, April trailing behind. April was younger, ten, eleven; small and skinny next to her sister's bulk. Her T-shirt was clean but blotchy with old stains, and her fingers were raw, the nails chewed down past the quick. Her nose was raw, too—a summer cold, allergies?

"Hi," she said, smiling shyly, catching up, and Susanna found herself smiling back, the lump slightly shrinking. April obviously wasn't anybody to be afraid of. In fact, she reminded Susanna a little bit of Megan, with her old friend's dark curly hair and triangular face. Not that Megan had ever been shy. Megan could talk happily to anybody: college students, old men walking their dogs, the lady with the stud in her nose who did tattoos. Anybody.

It was Melody who was still talking here. "You're probably wondering why we're bowling in the middle of the summer, but I tell you, there's not much to do around here. Reverend McGill tried to get a youth center going on Friday nights, you know, Ping-Pong, volleyball, food, just a place to hang out. But the kids who drive, they're out of here, and kids like us, there aren't many close enough to walk. And the parents get enough driving during the week, they're not interested. You guys are slow, come on. Let's cross while the crossing's good."

The main road was wider, curving off in both directions, empty. And then, suddenly, a car was coming fast, its horn blaring, the boys inside grinning, gesticulating. A beer can bounced along the gravel, and April, scurrying, grabbed for

Susanna's hand. Safely across, the three girls huddled, breathless. "Kasperzak," Melody said. "He's such a jerk." But her eyes glinted, triumphant. They'd been noticed. "Was that his brother with him? He's in your class, isn't he, April? Lonnie?"

"Only because he's flunked twice," said April. She sneezed, then sneezed again. "You got a tissue?" she said, but Melody was already rummaging in her knapsack.

"Here," she said, handing a wad to her sister, "but that's all I've got, so make them last. She's allergic to everything," she said to Susanna. "Pollen, dust, cats, what else, April?"

"Molds," April said. Her nose was even redder now. "And I can't eat peanuts or chocolate or strawberries. I get hives."

"Yeah, she's something," said Melody proudly. "Now me, I'm allergic, too. To food, right? But I just get fat." Her hands were on her hips now, her eyes appraising. "You sure are quiet. I just get fat, right? You're supposed to laugh."

But it wasn't funny. Why was she supposed to laugh if it wasn't funny? Susanna found she was staring right into Melody's face, shaking her head, shaking, and then Melody's eyes narrowed and she shrugged.

"Okay," she said. "So don't. We better get going. There's the van. Reverend McGill will want to meet you, and so will the other guys. Look, April, Tracy's there. I can't believe it, maybe she broke up with Dave. Wait'll you meet *her*," she said to Susanna. "You've got to like *her*, she's the most popu-lar—"

And then she saw Susanna's face and stopped short. "Hey," she said, and then more softly, "are you okay? You look . . . April, you run on ahead, tell them we're coming."

Popular. Susanna knew all about popular. If Melody was bad, impossible to say the right thing to, this Tracy would be worse. Tracy would take one look at Susanna, just like Amanda had that last time, and know that Susanna was nothing. Even though Susanna came from some fancy town far away with museums and bookstores and neat little shops, Tracy would understand immediately that she didn't know *anything*: the right groups, the right songs, the in clothes, the in look. After about ten words with Tracy, Susanna wouldn't even exist.

And boys. Susanna could see boys in front of the church, too, milling around the van, pushing at each other, laughing. Boys, she couldn't talk to boys, and then they'd all expect her to bowl, too, and she couldn't bowl, and they'd think she was the stupidest . . . she'd make such a fool . . . And then she was digging into the pocket of her jeans, her fingers fastening on paper, the five-dollar bill, she was shoving it toward Melody.

"Here, for the collection, whatever. I've got to . . . I'm sick, I'm sorry, I've got to go home, I'm sick."

"Hey," said Melody. "Listen! Can I . . . ?" But Susanna was running, across the main road and down her own, her feet crunching, pounding. Home, she had to get home. But where *was* home, where *was* someplace safe? And tomorrow her father would ask her, bowling, how was bowling, you didn't *go*? But how rude that is, Susanna, how rude. He'd grab, like everybody grabbed now, and then let go, disappointed that nothing they wanted was there.

The garage was empty, the car gone. That's right. They'd gone to a movie, found a theater ten miles away. Mike, too, grumbling, but there was nothing else to do on a Saturday night around here. Thank you, she thought, gulping for air. I don't have to see them, thank you. The garage was dim, almost cool, more a barn than garage; it had a loft even, stairs. She climbed, feeling warmer again in the rising heat, and something crunched underfoot. Flies. Shuddering, she knocked against a chain, the chain to a bare bulb. She pulled it, and light, shadow, swung up, then down. Up, then down. There was a table, some wooden chairs, a pile of boxes. Some tires, a shovel, stuff. She sat down.

Maybe she *was* sick. Maybe she was . . . say it. Sick in the head. Crazy. People *were* crazy: that lady on the bus at home, talking to herself; the old man in the park, eyes red, staring. Not normal. Yesterday she'd thought, I'm like Melody. Like Melody. But she wasn't. Melody had friends, bowled, took care of her little sister. She wasn't like Melody at all.

She jarred the table, and something rolled, an old ballpoint pen. FENTON'S FEED, it said in blue letters, its ink almost dried, but not quite. Paper? Why do people keep them, catalogs, old phone books, a bag full of other bags, brown grocery bags, folded. She pulled one out.

Without even thinking, she drew a line. She stared down at it, and then, very slowly, drew another. But her hand was moving by itself. It wasn't really drawing, it didn't count, didn't matter if it was good or bad. What was it going to be, even? Sometimes she didn't know when she started, until the lines told her. Would they tell her this time? Could they, after so long?

It seemed, growing under her hand, to be a cage. Yes, it was, a cage with a tree in one corner, a tree with long jutting branches, just right for . . . for what? For monkeys, it seemed. Yes, it was a cage for monkeys, but the monkey her fingers were making was small and there was something wrong with it. Oh, God, it didn't have a tail! Yes, it was dangling from one paw, from the tree, but it was almost falling. It was going to fall because it didn't have a tail, it needed a tail. *How can you hang on if you're missing a tail?*

Something dripped onto the paper. But her hand kept moving. It wasn't done, there was something else higher in the tree, another monkey, bigger. It was hanging upside down, long arms reaching, reaching down, almost. . . . Could it? Make the fingers longer, look up, little monkey, look up, see them, grab them, hang on. *Hang on.*

The little monkey reached up and hung on. Before Susanna dropped the pen, crying now too much to see, she realized that it wasn't just the little monkey that didn't have a tail.

The big monkey didn't either.

Chapter 7

"Uncle Louie?" She'd knocked twice and pushed open the door, but the room was empty. Was he in the bathroom? But the door was ajar, and there was no sound of running water. There was no sound at all.

Susanna stood very still and looked at the wall of pictures. Most of them, she saw now, were drawings. A few were washed with delicate color, but mostly they were black and white, some with harsh jagged lines, but more clean and spare. Some she recognized, a da Vinci or two, a Rembrandt. But others must be Uncle Louie's. Which ones? Soon she'd find out. Soon she'd know.

But not now. Right now, the pictures could wait. Even the rich, ordered clutter of the room hardly registered as she took another step. "Uncle Louie?" she called again. Please, she thought, please. Where are you? I need you. There was no answer, but the French door was ajar, too, just slightly. When she pulled it farther and stepped onto the balcony, she let out the breath she hadn't even known she was holding. He was there. He was sitting with his back to her, facing the trees, slumped down into his chair, unmoving. "Uncle Louie," she whispered. "Please?"

His head came suddenly up. "Who?" he said, turning. "*Who?*"

"It's okay, see, it's just me." His eyes followed her as she made her way around his chair. Then, as she moved to lean against the high railing, his hand shot out and grabbed the bottom of her T-shirt.

"Watch out!"

She froze. "What?"

"There! Don't bump it, you'll bump it." He let her go and pointed a shaking hand toward a corner of the balcony.

"What is it?" she said, and then she saw what it was. "A spider's web." She squatted down to look. It was large, lumpy with repairs and dust and insects; a working web. It looked like it had been there a long time.

"Where's the spider?" she asked. There was a sudden movement of something back into the space between the railing and the deck.

"There!" he repeated. "You see her? The web is her life. Her life. You won't wreck it, will you? You won't. . . ."

"I won't wreck it," said Susanna. She sat down, her movements controlled, careful, and slowly his hand came down into his lap. He sighed, and then Susanna sighed, too, and leaned back against the railing. It was cool up here, green, the high space surrounded by gently stirring trees. She took in another deep breath and let it out again, feeling the tears dry, the tension drain away.

Uncle Louie was looking at his hand now, turning it back and forth, back and forth, caught by something he couldn't seem to understand. Then his face cleared. "Yes," he said, more to himself than to Susanna. "I was little, yes. And we had a sandbox, Mary and me, our uncle made it, and a lid for it, to keep out the cats. So every time we wanted to play, we had to slide off the lid and prop it up. It was very heavy. We were only little, you see. And one day I said no, no, I can do it myself. I want to do it myself. Not you, Mary, me, and I pulled it up as high as I could, and then I dropped it." He splayed out his fingers. "That's where it fell, right there, nothing broke but the skin, you can see it, the scar. Can you see it?"

Susanna leaned over. She saw it, a faint white line drawn raggedly over three fingers. "Yes," she said. "Does it still hurt?"

"No," he said. His hand formed a fist and then dropped again into his lap. "It doesn't hurt." His gaze was on her face now, puzzled. "I forget. Who you are again?"

She flinched. And then she realized she hadn't really told him yesterday. "Susanna," she said. "I think I'm your niece. Your grandniece. And you're my great-uncle." She felt better, saying it, naming the connection. Because there was a connection. She could feel it.

"Great," he said. "Grand. Are you . . . grand?"

"No," said Susanna. She thought of a staircase, wide, curving, a chandelier brilliant overhead, glittering. "No." The floor of the deck was hard, gritty, but she didn't mind. For the first time in months, she felt safe. Like the spider. She pulled her knees up and held them. "My mother said you were an artist. I . . . that's what I like, too. Did you always want it? Want to paint?"

"What?" He sounded confused. "Paint?" He flexed his hands again, dropped them. "No." He frowned. "Not paint. Lines. I liked lines, you know. In the sand, fingers. Chalk on the sidewalk. Pencils."

Inside Susanna, something loosened even further. She knew about lines. "I drew in my cereal," she said. "And mashed potatoes."

His eyes brightened. "Yes," he said, nodding at her. "Mashed potatoes. Mashed potatoes . . . a fork . . ."

"And squash," said Susanna. "Thanksgiving is good. You don't think that's weird, wanting to do that? Crazy?"

"Crazy?" he said. He frowned again. "*He* thought . . . And *him* . . . Jealous. That's all. Jealous."

"Jealous?" said Susanna. That was a new thought to her, jealous. "Do you mean . . . ?"

He interrupted her. "Cream of Wheat," he said.

"What?" It was hard keeping track, his mind jumped around so much.

"Cereal, you said. Cream of Wheat, with a spoon, I'd like that."

"You want me to make you Cream of Wheat? Now? With milk?"

"Of course not with milk. *You* know, a spoon, a little sugar, just a sprinkle."

Susanna got up. "Cream of Wheat," she said, and she grinned. She had to. Because crazy, here was crazy. Not scary crazy, though. Funny crazy. Or sad, maybe. Maybe both. "But you have to eat it," she said.

He grunted.

"You have to promise," she said.

"Maybe," he finally said. "After . . ." She nodded. After the lines.

"You'd better," she said.

There was a box in the pantry, half full. The drawers all stuck, swollen, but yanking, Susanna found measuring cups, a wooden spoon. She pulled a pan from the jumble in the cupboard next to the oven, no lid, but she didn't need one. You had to stir.

She'd turned on the light over the sink but the stove was dim, the gas flame blue. Pallid, grainy, the Cream of Wheat burped, slowly thickened. She dipped a finger, no taste really, that's why sugar, just a sprinkle, he'd said. But which bowl? This was important. Guess wrong and he'd say, no, I don't want it.

She guessed right. Upstairs, he ran a finger slowly around the rim. It was blue, chipped on one side. "Mary did that. He couldn't blame me, not that time."

"Who?"

"Him." His hand on the spoon trembled, traced a line, stopped. "He'd never let me. Eat it, he'd say. Don't mess. You're messing in it again!" His hand jerked as though slapped, and the spoon dropped.

"Your father?" What had her mother said about Grandpa Grinell? Safely dead. That's what her mother had said. Uncle Louie hadn't come home until his father was safely dead.

"It's okay, Uncle Louie," she said. "I'll let you. Here." But he pushed the bowl away, fists clenched. She fingered the spoon with its scalloped handle, old-dime thin, tarnished. It was silver. Beautiful. Her hand, by itself, dipped and offered. "Here," she said. "You promised."

He looked up at her, and slowly his scowl faded. "Grand," he said. "*She* was grand. Your hair is just like hers . . . but you said you were someone else."

"Susanna," she whispered.

"That's right. Susanna. You liked my room. 'Oh, Susanna,' " he sang softly, " 'oh, don't you cry for me.' Yes. I won't forget, now. It's a nice name, Susanna."

His eyes were closed now, but his mouth stayed open like a small bird waiting to be fed. He swallowed the spoonful she was holding, then another. He ate it all. Susanna cradled the empty bowl, light now, so light it might rise, fly, hang glowing in the night sky, become a star. Her star it would be, hers and Uncle Louie's. She had made it, he had eaten it. Theirs.

She noticed everything at once. It was almost dark, but his face against the white wicker gave off a last pale shimmer. It was bristled, unshaven. His hair was uncombed, his fingernails dirty. A stale smell came off him of clothes worn too long. And the deck under her feet needed sweeping. Yes, she had been right this morning. Uncle Louie had stopped caring, because with Mary gone, he felt that nobody really cared about *him*.

But she cared. And because she did, he had eaten. If she cared enough, maybe he could do more. Work again. Live again. She had come to him for help, and she *had* been helped. He'd recognized her, talked to her, trusted her. And her picture, her first picture in months? Hadn't she been thinking of him when she drew it? Yes. In her picture, it hadn't just been the little monkey reaching up to be saved. It had been the big monkey reaching down.

Chapter 8

Two days later, Susanna vacuumed the last square foot of Uncle Louie's floor, switched off the cleaner, and collapsed onto the wide geometric border of the rug nearest the French doors. This time she didn't even notice it. She couldn't: too much sweat was dripping into her eyes. The rest of her felt marinated, coated with a thin even mix of moisture and salt and dirt. Wasn't there a beetle that oozed stuff? Sticky? Shiny? She felt like that.

But good, too. From where she lay she could just see the top of Uncle Louie's head. He was sitting in his usual wicker chair on the balcony, just as he had two nights ago. But now his hair was combed, his face shaven, his fingernails clean. She'd done that. Well, she hadn't done it, he had, but only because she'd set everything out for him, plugged in his razor, put toothpaste on his toothbrush, found his comb where it had dropped down behind the toilet. She'd run a bath for him and taken clean clothes from the wardrobe, the rich pattern of its inlaid panels a reward under her fingers.

Many rewards. He'd eaten something from every tray she brought him. Not much, maybe, but something: soup, mashed potatoes, ice cream. Soft things like Cream of Wheat. Both mornings his cereal bowl had been scraped clean, his mouth opening, accepting, swallowing what she spooned up for him. Maybe she'd make him egg salad for lunch today. And applesauce. She bet he'd eat a nice cool dish of applesauce right up.

He didn't seem to mind her cleaning, either. Yesterday, after lunch, he'd sat in the chair behind his heavy round table and watched her dust. Just the bookcases had taken her the whole afternoon because she kept having to stop. For a while, he'd shared her pleasure at what he called his zoo, the animals of ebony and ivory, bone and wood, stone and pottery that served as bookends. His favorite was a terra-cotta fox on the top shelf. It lay curled and compact under a copper lamp: sharp-nosed, bright-eyed, gleaming. She'd lifted it carefully down to be petted before she dusted it and put it back.

And the books! Pictures kept leaping out at her from them: every artist, every museum she'd ever heard of, and many she hadn't. She'd felt dizzy, stunned. "Oh, Uncle Louie," she'd breathed, "look, who *is* this?" But finally his eyes had closed. "Tired," he'd said. He'd slept. In the silence, the books had piled around her, too much, too much. Finally she'd shut her own eyes and just dusted.

This morning she'd done the picture wall with a long-handled mop, sneezing. It must have been years since her grandmother had done it, the dust had sifted down like rain. "Dusting?" her mother had said. "You hate dusting." But this was different. This work was for Uncle Louie and her. She'd stopped only once, when she'd reached the bottom row. The drawings were small there, almost miniature; a series, a house surrounded by trees. This house, but from years ago, with some trees new, some no longer there. Twelve pictures, twelve months, spare lines catching changing leaves, changing light. They were beautiful. Squatting, squinting, she'd seen initials. L.C.G. They were his.

Quickly, then, she'd scanned the other rows, hopeful of spotting more—bigger works, later works, twenty years' worth. No. Well, they were stored someplace, probably. Or sold. She'd ask him later, she'd thought. Soon, now, when the bathroom and balcony were done. Soon, now, after she finished.

Then he'd be clean, clean and comfortable and eating again. It had been only two days. She hadn't known she could do so much in just two days. Yes, soon, during long cool evenings on the balcony, watching the stars coming out, they'd talk. He hadn't said much so far, but that would change. He was getting to know her, getting used to having her around. Friendship took time, you couldn't just force it like Melody had tried to. Not that Melody would probably try again, after Saturday. But she didn't want Melody, did she? No, she'd make her own friends. "She doesn't have any friends," Mike had said, but he was wrong. She had Uncle Louie.

And together, she and Uncle Louie would . . . what? Wonderful images had bloomed in her head as she'd cleaned: the two of them not only talking but working, encouraging each other. Uncle Louie teaching her everything he knew, releasing her to do the kind of work she *knew*—

Somebody knocked and the door swung open. "Susanna?"

Susanna scrambled to her feet.

"Hey, babe, you look like you could use a break." Her father looked, turned, looked some more. "Your mother was right. He's got some beautiful stuff, doesn't—"

Hardly knowing what she was doing, Susanna pushed her father out into the hall and shut the door behind them. *My room!* She was trembling and had to steady herself against the wall. "You can't . . ." she started and then took a deep breath. "Didn't Mom tell you? He's afraid."

"Afraid of me?" said her father. "Do I look dangerous? What am I going to do, hit him over the head with this?" He raised his clarinet. He'd been practicing, and his face, too, was damp with sweat.

"Of men," she said.

"Well, it's lucky he can find so many women to wait on him then, isn't it? I wonder if I could pull that off, lock myself in my room when—"

"Leave him alone!" Blurted out, it shocked them both.

She'd never talked to her father in that tone of voice. "Sorry," she said. "But he's . . . different, Dad."

"Yeah," he said. "I know. And it's good to see you helping out. But . . ." He ran a finger over the smooth throat of his mouthpiece and then shook his head. "Nothing's simple, is it? Good to help Uncle Louie, your mom, but don't . . ."

"What?"

"I'm not sure. Expect too much, maybe. Invest too much. He's an old man, Susie."

"Mom said he's only sixty. That's not old. That guy you perform with in the pit orchestra sometimes—he's eighty something, isn't that what you said, and he's great?"

"Carl? Yeah, he is. He *is* great. Eighty-four and he's still got it. But there's old and old, Susie. Louie, here, locking himself away, well, you know it's not exactly the best way to live a life. I'm not saying we all aren't tempted, sometimes. There've been times, if a cliff had been handy, I would have tossed this clarinet right off it. Right? But I didn't. The point is, giving up like that just doesn't work. You've got to keep going, slog things out. Not walk into a room and slam the door."

Susanna stared silently at the floor. He was trying to understand, she knew that, but she just didn't want to listen to him right now. She wanted to get back to Uncle Louie. Besides, she wasn't sure he *was* right. Wasn't a slammed door sometimes the best answer when everything you needed was behind it?

She heard her father sigh. "Right," he said. "Well, I didn't mean to get into all of this now. That girl just called, Melody? She wanted to know if you were feeling better, said you should call her back. I didn't know you were sick."

She felt sick now. Nothing's simple, he'd said, but it was worse than that. Things were getting so tangled and knotted that she couldn't take a step without tripping. "I'm not," she said.

"Did something happen at bowling? It couldn't have been easy, going. I remember—"

"No." Say it. "I didn't go bowling."

"You didn't go bowling."

"No."

"Susanna, your mother asked you about bowling; you said it was fine."

"It probably was fine. For them." She wished she could explain, tell him, but she couldn't. So why couldn't he just leave it, why had he started pushing now like everybody else? Under her hand the china knob felt cool, smooth, and she could almost see him, Uncle Louie, sitting clean and quiet on his balcony.

"I have to finish practicing before lunch," he said. "We'll talk about this then. I don't like it, Susanna. There's lots of ways to lie, you know, and I don't like any of them."

She turned the knob, pushed open the door.

"And Susanna," he said. He hadn't moved, but she was almost through the door, almost. "You'll call that girl back this afternoon. Do you understand?"

He didn't understand. But she nodded, once. She heard his footsteps start down the hall and shut the door behind them.

Chapter 9

Uh, is, uh, Melody there?"

"Who is this?" The voice was a man's, impatient, and Susanna could hear something clattering in the background. A dog started barking, somebody laughed, and then there was a blare of voices, as though a TV had been turned up loud.

"I, uh, my name's Susanna. Mrs. Grahame up the road, she was my grandmother and—"

But the phone had already been dropped. "Hey! Mel! Get this and get off! I'm expecting a call." The voice receded, rose, ". . . that nosy old . . ." receded again.

"Hello?" Melody was almost whispering, breathing hard.

"Uh, Melody? This is Susanna. My dad said . . ."

"Listen," said Melody. "I can't talk now, okay? They're going camping, I have to help get stuff ready. Could you come over later? Around three, maybe three-thirty? April . . ." The receiver fell again. "Hey!" Susanna heard, then a grunt, then, muffled, "Hey, just a minute, okay?" Finally, Melody again, hoarse now in her ear. "Three-thirty, okay?"

"Uh," began Susanna. The dead phone buzzed in her ear. She listened to it for a long moment and then hung it up. Right. Three-thirty. And she'd have to go. It didn't matter to any of them that she'd been going to make tea for Uncle Louie at three-thirty: iced tea with sliced lemon in the tall frosted glasses she'd seen in her grandmother's pantry. Sitting on the balcony, swept clean except for the spider, they would have sipped it and looked through Uncle Louie's books and talked about how it was, art, and how it made you see things, feel things differently from other people.

Her parents just didn't seem to understand how important all this was. If she could help Uncle Louie, become his friend, she would get her art back. She knew she would. Together, neither of them had to be afraid anymore. Of being lonely. Of failing. Together they couldn't fail.

Like she would fail with Melody. Susanna squeezed her eyes shut, squeezing out the thought, concentrating instead on a clean, small room with a clean, small canvas. If she concentrated hard enough she could almost feel the charcoal under her hand, see the canvas, white and cool . . .

"Hey. Wake up. You done? I got to make a call."

Mike didn't look clean, small, cool. He'd finished his scraping and was painting now. His face was beet red under the bill of his cap, his arms and hands blotched white.

Susanna surfaced slowly, blinking. "You're calling Kim in the middle of the day? Dad'll kill you."

"Look, not that it's any of your business, but I'm paying for it, okay? So, out."

Out. Uncle Louie's room had completely faded now and in its place stood Melody and the reality of the afternoon that lay ahead. Melody. Suddenly, instinctively, Susanna grabbed Mike's arm. Help me, she thought. Because he used to help her. Like that time down by the lake, wading, when she'd stepped on that sharp rock, and he'd wound his towel around her foot and almost killed himself lugging her back to the car. And when she'd been studying for that spelling bee and he'd leapt out at her from every corner of the house. "Persevere! Prevaricate! Puissance! Puissance? What the—" and she'd laughed so hard she couldn't even spell her own name.

There was no point, though, to memories like that. All they did was hurt. She dropped his arm before he could shake her hand off, but there was one thing she couldn't stop herself from asking. "Why don't you like me anymore?" she said.

"What? Oh, come on, Suz." But he looked more wary than mad, glanced into her face, away. "What are you talking about?"

"You used to. Now it's like I'm garbage, I smell, like you wish I'd just crawl into a plastic bag and . . ." And now Susanna felt the pain start to ratchet her voice up, up. Soon she'd be out of control.

"Come on, don't talk so crazy, I—"

"*I'm not crazy!*"

"Okay, okay, I didn't mean it like that, it's just . . ." He looked at the phone miserably, longingly. "Look, I still like you, okay? It's just, I wish . . . you'd . . . get a life. You know? Get some new friends, get . . . happy again. I mean, it's scary, watching you just totally flip out because Amanda—"

"*Who told you about Amanda?*"

"Nobody told me, I got eyes. She dumped you, right? Well, so maybe I don't like seeing what can happen to people when other people do that to them."

Susanna couldn't believe what she was hearing. "You think it's catching? You think you, the big football star, could ever be like—"

"Shut up!" They stared at each other and then Mike, as though he saw something he couldn't stand, turned away and picked up the phone. "Look, Kim took her driver's test this morning, okay, and I got to see if she passed. Okay?" He hunched over, dialing, pretending she'd already left, and just his fingers going through the motions seemed enough to wipe away his words, his anger . . . Susanna. "Hi, Kim? How'd it go? Yeah? All right!"

Susanna banged the kitchen door behind her and plopped down on the steps. Why had she thought even for a second that he might understand? How could he, when things were so simple for him? Things had always been simple for him. He'd been born switched on, so there was always something flowing, some kind of energy going between him and other people. Even when he was slamming around, mad about something or with somebody, he could do that, because it wouldn't really hurt. Nothing could as long as the hum was there, the power was on. Her mother was like that, too.

Susanna had gone once, when she was little, to her mother's class, and watched her connect, minute after minute, hour after hour with all those kids, those poor kids. Her mother would talk and cry and yell and laugh, and those kids would talk and cry and yell and laugh right back. Susanna had had to force herself just to say hello.

Okay, okay, why did she keep going over and over and over it, what was the point? She was different, she was a freak, but so was Uncle Louie, and remember, reaching up, reaching down, remember. . . . She took a deep breath, let it out again. Calm. Just be calm. Just go over to Melody's, be polite, don't panic, do what you have to do and come back. Uncle Louie will be waiting for you. He had accepted who he was and made it work and she would, too. She'd learn to be herself and she'd be okay.

What was her mother doing? Feeling slightly better, Susanna plumped down a couple more steps and craned to see the side of the house. Her mother had propped open the door to the screened porch and was shaking something. She saw Susanna and waved. "Come see this," she called. "It's fabulous."

It was a cloak. Susanna sank onto the grass and her mother

piled it into her lap, folds and folds, silky and silvery. It *was* fabulous.

"It has a hood," her mother said. "See? Just like those hooded cloaks on the front of those gothic novels." Romantic, she meant, but it was more than that. It was protection: nothing could hurt you wearing something like this. "It must be a hundred years old. I think it was my mother's grandmother's; there's a picture somewhere. An evening cloak, for dancing. Can't you just see this with a ball gown, diamonds? Imagine being handed into a coach?" She sighed. "Not much use for it now. It doesn't fit me anyway. I'm too short. It might fit you, in a year or two, if you want it."

Yes. Susanna nodded. "Thanks," she said.

Her mother stood, hovered, then sighed again. "Okay, then. Good. Susanna, look, your dad . . ."

"I'm going to see her," said Susanna. "At three-thirty. I called her."

"He just wants . . ." Her mother stopped, shook her head. "He's afraid . . ." Another shake, impatient. "It's just that he knows what it's like to feel . . . stuck. And he doesn't want you to stay stuck, you know, to give up. He, we, want you to keep trying, even though it hurts, because you've got so much talent. So much to give.

"Yeah, yeah, you don't believe me, do you? Nobody believes parents. Now, Megan, you always believed Megan. I can still hear her shrieking about some great project you'd cooked up, and you grinning. Boy, I miss Megan. Letters—

they're just no substitute for the real thing, are they? Well, I miss Amanda, too, but I could see that one coming, her moving on to other things. No, it was you and Megan that kept things boiling. Amanda was fine, I liked Amanda. But Amanda was just along for the ride."

Susanna sat staring at her, trying to take it all in. For months, nobody had even mentioned Amanda's name. It was like Amanda never existed the way they'd all ignored, pretended to ignore, the way she'd disappeared. Why, now, were they all beginning to talk about her, give advice, now when Susanna had found Uncle Louie and didn't need Amanda anymore, or some kind of replacement from down the road?

But her mother was waiting for an answer. So what did she want to hear? Susanna sighed. "It's okay, Mom," she said. "I'm okay." And then, because her mother still stood there, and because one thing she'd said, the last thing, had been something Susanna wouldn't mind hearing again, she said it herself. "Did you really mean that? That Amanda was just . . . along for the ride."

"I guess I thought you always knew," her mother said. "I guess I took it for granted. Took way too many things for granted, maybe, instead of saying them." She squatted down beside Susanna and gave her a hard hug. "I *know* you're okay. Or will be. You're my daughter, aren't you? And we're tough stock, we Grahame women. Your grandmother, me, you . . . we don't give up easily." She stood, then, squaring her shoulders, and when she spoke again, her voice was brisk.

"I'd better get back to Grandma's clothes. You might want

to go through some of the piles when I'm done. She saved some stuff from the fifties, it's probably all back in now. Hey, you could be the hit of the ninth grade."

Her mother was sure right about one thing. She didn't give up easily. Was Susanna like her, more like her than she'd ever thought? "Mom?" she blurted. "I really like the cloak. I'm really glad you gave it to me."

Her mother leaned against the porch door she was holding, and looked down at her. Then she smiled. "Thank you, sweetie," she said. "Thank you. I'm glad."

Chapter 10

Melody was waiting at her door, and when she saw Susanna, she stepped out and let it slam behind her. "I'd invite you in, but it's kind of a pit," she said. "Well, it *is* a pit, and it's worse now with all the stuff Tommy dragged out to take and then Dad wouldn't let him. I don't know why they *go* camping, all they do is yell at each other. Maybe it's better when they get there. You want to go down to the creek?"

"I can't stay very long," said Susanna. "But, yeah, okay." The yard was a pit, too; she could see again what her mother meant. Why did they have all that stuff there? Bikes, okay, and the posts for a badminton net except there wasn't any net. But a dryer? An old sink? The whole bathroom, actually. Melody kicked at the toilet as she went by.

"Those were supposed to go in the shed—you never know when you might need something, right—but then it burned. We go down here, watch out, it's kind of steep. Lisa wants to put some steps in. Yeah, well, maybe when hell freezes over." Susanna followed her, clutching at weeds, sliding the last few feet. This time Melody didn't move so fast, breathing hard, winded. She was still in jeans, a big sweater, she must be boiling. How was she going to get back up?

"Okay," said Melody. "Okay, it'll be easier now. Over here."

So far, anyway, Susanna didn't feel as nervous as she'd thought she would. Actually, she even felt a little curious; Melody's family seemed so weird. "Who's Lisa?" she asked. It wasn't really a path they were on, just trampled down weeds, but pretty weeds with blue starry flowers delicate against bumpy stalks.

Watercolor, Susanna thought instinctively, and for the first time in months didn't feel her stomach clutch at the thought of actually putting something down on paper. Even *she* couldn't go too wrong with weeds. She rubbed her fingers together tentatively. Yes, for once it didn't feel scary, that itch for a brush. If she could maybe find some of these flowers behind her grandfather's house, maybe she and Uncle—

"Lisa? My dad's girlfriend, she's not bad. I'm kind of hoping she sticks around longer than the last one. My . . . uh, my mom died." Melody had been plowing ahead, grass thwapping against her legs, but now she stopped. "I forgot, you're slow, aren't you? But then maybe you're still sick, like you were on Saturday. You didn't look sick, but then I figured maybe it was your period."

Susanna felt herself stiffen, the color wash up over her face. She should have known Melody would . . . But then, come on, why shouldn't Melody ask, it was a natural question, normal, normal people wouldn't get so . . .

"No," she said, because Melody was beginning to turn around. "No, I'm okay. You said there was a creek?"

"Just down over here. You've seen your part, haven't you? It goes down behind your place, too, before it crosses the road. Really, you haven't been back there? This is my favorite place. Me and April come down here all the time. See?"

Susanna saw. It was a wide creek, running fast over rocks. It was bright and cool, both: buoying up, calming down. All opposites were caught here, contained in the rapid broken movement. Not even knowing how she got there, Susanna squatted at the edge, a tiny beach of gravel made for getting close, for touching. The water, rippling over her fingers, was warmer than it looked.

"It's nice, isn't it?" Melody, eager, squatted clumsily beside her. "You can wade here, and then, down farther, we kind of dammed it up, not really, but it's deep enough to sit in when the creek's high. I mean, you can't swim, but it's cool. Sometimes . . ." She looked around. "I even, you know, skinny-dip. Nobody else ever comes down here; it's great." She shifted, silence, more silence, then her voice roughened. "Melody the hippo, right? Like in those African movies, wal-

lowing around. Great White Whale, my dad says sometimes;
here comes the Great White—"

"No." Susanna fingered a stone. It felt smooth like a china
doorknob, like the one to Uncle Louie's room. But she wasn't
in Uncle Louie's room. She was here. Melody's finger was
poking hard into the gravel. Hurt yourself before they hurt
you. Susanna knew all about that. "I mean, I wasn't thinking
that," she said. "I was thinking how nice it would feel. All
I've ever swum in was pools."

Beside her, Melody slowly relaxed, sank back on her
haunches, sat. "The only pool around here is at the high
school. Well, some people have those above-ground ones, but
not anybody I know. My friend, Coreen, well she's kind of a
friend, she lives on a farm two, three miles down the road.
They've got a pond, but it's muddy, the bottom's mud and the
cows go there, too."

"Yuck," said Susanna and grinned. She couldn't help it.

Melody's eyes brightened and she grinned back. "Yeah,"
she said. "It's gross. But I go there sometimes. Her brother,
Coreen's brother, Randy, I think he kind of likes me. You've
probably got a boyfriend, right?"

Again, Susanna's face flamed. Oh, sure. Sure she did.
Right. And it wasn't even as though she didn't see . . . didn't
want. . . . The image came to her clearly, the boy next to her
in art class last year, his fingers tight on charcoal, his muscles
tense with effort from the wrist to where his arm disappeared
into cloth. He wore blue T-shirts, dark blue and black. He'd

asked her once about an assignment, but she'd just shaken her head that she didn't know, except she did. It had been right after Amanda, so what would have been the point? No point. No point at all. "No," she said, and stood up. "I've got to go."

Melody heaved herself slowly to her feet. "Really? Already? Well, hey, how long are you guys going to be here? All summer, or what? Lisa said she heard your grandfather might be selling out."

"I don't know," said Susanna.

Silence. Then Melody spoke. "See," she said, "my thing is, I don't give up." She stood, huge, solid, unmoving, hands on hips. "Because of my mom, right? She was real sick, she was big like me, like I am now, but at the end, I was only ten and I could've probably picked her up. But she made them keep trying things, trying to make her better. April was only six." Her voice faltered for a minute, then forged stubbornly ahead. "So she said to me, Melody—she never called me Mel, it was always Melody—Melody, she said, you give up, you get nothing. Nothing. So maybe you don't like me, but you might, like the creek, you didn't think you'd like that, but you did."

"It's not . . ." And then Susanna felt something soften, suddenly, like a mold dipped in warm water releasing gelatin, letting it slide out, right side up, onto a plate. Thoughts into words, slipping right out. "It's not you. It's me. I used to know how to be friends, at least I thought I did, but I was wrong, I'm too weird. I don't think right; I can't talk.

Whatever I say, it's wrong. I can't do it anymore. It's too hard. But it's not you." She finally looked up.

Melody's eyes were intent, her head cocked, like an animal listening to something stirring out beyond the woods, far off in a back pasture. She was listening hard. She heard me, Susanna thought suddenly. And then Melody nodded. "That's okay, then," she said. "I mean, you don't have much to lose, do you, practicing on me?"

Practice. That's what her father had said about Uncle Louie. Practice. But Melody too? She looked at the older girl again, patient, waiting. "I guess not," she said slowly.

"Okay, then," said Melody. "It's supposed to be hot again, tomorrow. You want to come over after lunch, bring your suit? We could splash around down here. April will probably come too, but you don't have to worry about April, she likes you."

"She does?" Susanna remembered April's small hand, clutching at her own, crossing the road. Reaching for her, trusting.

"April likes everybody," said Melody. "Too much, sometimes. That's why she needs me." She started up the small slope from the creek, breathing hard already. "When my mom was sick, she said, 'Melody, you look after April. You take care of her.' Not my dad, not Tommy, she knew Tommy'd be lucky if he could graduate high school, and she was right. He was eleven then; he's sixteen now and he just quit."

She stopped so suddenly Susanna bumped into her,

smelling sweat but over it, working hard against it, some kind of perfume. Melody was planted rock solid now, staring at the weeds under her feet. "Well, I'm going to graduate. And so is April. See, she doesn't even know she has to fight, but that's okay. I do, and I'll fight okay, I'll fight for us both. That's what Mom knew. She knew I could do it. It's just that some-times . . . it gets hard sometimes. . . . I get, I don't know, I get . . . lonely."

Susanna could hardly hear the last word. But she heard it. She heard it. And then, she didn't know how, it seemed to sink into her, "lonely," to push something, to start something up. Or to *pull* something up, like you'd pull up a shade to let in the light. To let someone see.

And it was working. She *was* seeing again, seeing shapes forming, unrolling now in the old familiar effortless stream. These shapes were triangles, three of them, their points slowly blossoming into circles. Into . . . faces. Faces? Could she draw them? She stumbled to find the words. "Do you have a picture, you know, a photo? Of your mom?"

Melody turned, frowning. "Yeah. It's not very good. Why?"

Could she? It felt so good, images finally *there* again in her head, growing, growing, but could she really get them out? And if she could, would they be any good?

"I . . . I have to think. But I'll tell you tomorrow. I mean, if you can lend me the photo, maybe I can even show you. Except I've never tried people much, except you know, me. We had to do a self-portrait last year. . . ."

And then the old familiar words in her head, her teacher's voice. This is no *good*, Susanna. No good, no good, no good. . . .

But before they could echo any further, April appeared at the top of the slope. She waved, gave a great shriek of joy, and started sliding down toward them.

Chapter 11

Susanna! It's you! You're here! Oh, you're not going, are you? You can't!"

April, her eyes shining, stumbled the last few feet of the incline and, if Susanna hadn't reached out to grab her, would have fallen into a tangle of weeds. "Whoops!" she said. "Thanks!" Her pale pointed face was blotched with excitement, and it took Susanna a minute to remember that April had met her only two days ago for ten minutes and had hardly said a word. Now she was beaming like they'd been best friends forever.

But Susanna had to smile back. April really *was* a lot like Megan, brimming with energy and friendliness, and confidence that the world was a good place to be. Oh, Megan, she thought, and for the first time, it didn't really hurt to think of the friend who was so far away.

Now April was looking anxiously at her sister. "You didn't show her, did you, Melody? The clay, you didn't show her?"

"Relax," said Melody. "I didn't show her the clay." She raised an eyebrow at Susanna, but her voice was indulgent.

"Oh, Susanna, wait'll you see it!" said April. "It's a bank, this whole bank beside the creek I found last week, and it's great, come on, Melody, you thought so, too. It's better than that stuff at school, and we're going to make all kinds of things, you know, bowls, pots, just like the Indians—"

"April, she's got to go *home* now," said Melody, but threw Susanna a quizzical glance. "It really is pretty good, smooth, not a lot of junk in it, maybe tomorrow—"

"Not *tomorrow*," said April. "Oh, please, Susanna, now, come and look at it now. *Please?*"

"Well," said Susanna. But it was really too late now to give Uncle Louie tea, it was too close to his supper. And April's hand, slipped into hers just as it had two days ago, felt too trusting to just shake away. "Well, okay. I mean, sure. Where?"

April squeezed her fingers happily and started tugging Susanna after her through the weeds, Melody trundling along in their wake.

"You go down over here. I never used to like this way—I saw a snake, what was it, Melody, two years ago, and I was so afraid."

"Yeah, two years ago, but don't worry, Susanna, we haven't

seen any this year. And anyway my dad says the snakes around here won't hurt you. I mean, they're not poisonous or anything."

"That's okay," said Susanna. Touching, talking: with somebody like April it all felt so natural, so effortless. So unthreatening. "I kind of like snakes."

April turned, her eyes wide. "You do? Melody and me . . . ugh!"

"I didn't used to," said Susanna. "But in the sixth grade, this guy came to our school and he had these cages full of them, all different sizes and colors and we got to look at them and hold them."

"Yeah?" Melody looked impressed. "You've got more guts than I do, then."

"Not really. But he had this little one. It was so pretty. No, it *was*. The patterns on it and the way it moved, and it had this cute little tongue."

April suddenly screamed, "Snake! There! Watch out!" Susanna and Melody jumped, bumped, shrieked, and then they both saw that April was laughing, hugging herself gleefully.

"April fool!" she shouted.

"April," Melody began ominously, and her sister, seeing the blankness on Susanna's face, immediately wilted, her eyes anxious now, dismayed.

"I'm sorry, Susanna," she said. "You're not mad, are you? It's just, April fool, see, I can do that anytime, because my *name* is . . . Susanna, don't be mad."

Susanna took a deep breath, but the feeling rising up in her wasn't mad at all. Her words, April's shout, her shriek were all part of a bubble billowing quickly and lightly up inside her. It was a wonderful bubble, a silly bubble, and she hadn't felt silly for so long. It felt so good.

"I'll get you for that," she said, grinning, giving April a gentle sock on the arm. It was all coming back to her, the teasing, the mock anger; and Melody was part of it, too, so the words kept flowing, easy, unchecked. "You got to do something about this kid."

"I know," said Melody happily. She looked prettier all of a sudden, the tense lines in her face smoothed away. "You're baaaad, April." And then, as though not wanting to press their luck, "But Susanna can't hang around here all day. So come on. Show her where this great stuff is."

"Down here," said April. "Watch out, some of those rocks are loose. Then we have to go down the creek some. You don't mind getting your feet a little wet, Susanna, do you? It's around the bend, there, where the bank hangs over, see?"

The sun was hot on Susanna's back and the water, seeping up through her sneakers, was cold against her toes. But nice. They had to cross the creek, so instead of balancing on rocks, trying to avoid the burbling water, she followed Melody down into it. All three of them squished and splashed their way to the other side.

"See?" April said again. "I couldn't believe it when I found it. It's real clay, isn't it? See, you can use a rock like this to dig it out."

It *was* real clay, a dark gray smooth lump that softened as you worked it. April led them to a wide expanse of rock that splayed out into the shallow water, and plunked herself down. "I'm going to make beads with mine. I think there's a way you can bake them in the oven to get them hard. What are you going to make, Susanna?"

"I don't know," said Susanna.

"Me either," said Melody. "Mom used to get us that plasticine stuff, remember, April? But all I ever knew how to do was roll it out and then coil it up into a bowl. This stuff crumbles on me, though. It doesn't really work."

"I think you have to keep it wet," said Susanna. "We did some modeling in art a couple of years ago. I remember . . ." And it really didn't hurt to remember for once, the three of them, she and Megan and Amanda, all giggling when they started, but then settling, becoming intent as ideas formed under their hands. "I had these friends, this one, especially, Megan, and we were supposed to make animals, you know, like for an ark? But they could be imaginary? So I made blogs, they were these dumpy little birds with hardly any wings but great big feet. I mean *great* big feet, you could just see Noah trying to drag them onto the ark, it would take him all day.

"So Megan, she said okay, she'd make *blig*-blogs, like mine, right, only bigger? Well, *I* know, but you had to know her. She was really funny. So she made this enormous blog, and it took her so long that by the time she was done, all the clay was gone. And she needed two for the ark, right? Well, she just dug into the middle of it and pulled and pulled, and when she got done, she had two, all right. Then she told the teacher that the trouble with blig-blogs was sometimes they just blew blup!"

"Oh, man," said Melody, grinning. "Nothing like that ever goes on in *our* school."

"You're so lucky, Susanna," said April. "And look." She pointed to Susanna's hands. They had remembered, too, and were working on their own, building shapes up, smoothing them down. "You really know how to make stuff, I'll bet. Could you make something for me?"

"Sure," said Susanna. "What do you want?"

April didn't even have to think. "A cat," she said. "I love cats, and we can't have any because I'm so allergic."

"Well, I'll try," said Susanna. "A big cat, or a kitten?"

"A kitten, I guess," said April. "Everybody gives me cats, ceramic ones, you know; our room's full of them, isn't it, Melody? But I don't have too many kittens. Can you make it fluffy?"

"I'll try," Susanna said again, and was immediately oblivious to anything but the small figure forming in her hands.

Melody had already given up. She had taken off her sneakers and rolled up her jeans and was swishing her feet gently in the water. "We're almost behind your place here," she said. "Your grandfather's place. If you cross back over, all you have to do is climb the bank and look up and you can see the house. Your grandfather cut down some of the weeds there and brought down a bench. It's nice. I think they used to sit there, your grandmother and him, and sometimes your grandmother and, you know, *him*."

Susanna's fingers, pinching out an ear, almost pinched it off. "Uncle Louie?"

"Is that his name? She never said much about him, except that her brother lived with them and was kind of shy. We, everybody always wondered if there was something wrong. You know, if he was, well, disabled some way."

She stopped abruptly, but it was too late. Susanna felt the bubble inside her almost physically drop, then harden, then sink. Disabled? How dare Melody even *think* . . . With her fingernail, she fluffed up the clay fur and placed the finished kitten beside the row of April's beads. It was good, and under her anger she felt a stab of real pleasure, real pride before she plunked her feet back down into the creek bed. "All yours," she said. "I really have to go."

"Oh, Susanna," said April. "It's beautiful. How did you . . . ? Melody, look, it's really a kitten, I've never seen . . ."

But Melody had not only seen the change in Susanna's face, she'd heard her voice. "Hey," she said and shook her head. "Look. I'm sorry, I didn't mean . . ."

"Will you come back tomorrow?" asked April, gently stroking the little figure nestled in her hand. "Will you show me how to bake this, Susanna, and then you can see some of my other cats?"

"I don't know," said Susanna, and then, at April's puzzled

look, her voice softened. "There's stuff I might have to do."

"So yeah, okay," said Melody gruffly. "Look, then, I suppose you don't still want that photo?"

Susanna swayed, suddenly dizzy. Then she felt Melody's supporting hand and the spinning in her head steadied down to a familiar confusion. Was she really mad at Melody? Was there any point?

"Yes," she said. "I mean, no, I don't know." She shook her head and tried to smile. "I guess I don't know much anymore. But look. In the morning? Call me and I'll see."

Chapter 12

But the next morning when Melody called, her voice hoarse and rushed, it wasn't to ask anything but only to say that her father and brother had come home near dawn covered in mosquito bites. They'd forgotten their tent, and it would be better to lay low for a couple of days. "I'll call you, okay?" she whispered. "I gotta go."

Relief? Disappointment? Susanna picked up the breakfast tray she had set down to answer the phone and started up the stairs. Relief, maybe, except Melody had sounded strange, like she'd been crying, or trying not to cry, and Susanna didn't want to think about what it might take to make Melody cry. It would take a lot. She'd stayed here one night, she'd said, when her father . . . She hadn't finished. When her father what? Susanna, watching the Cream of Wheat slurp gently back and forth in its blue-rimmed bowl, suddenly felt sick.

Her own father was coming out of the bathroom. He looked damp and clean, his dark hair a cheerful tangle. "Morning, Susie," he said. "Your mom and I are going to visit a couple of the school districts today, just to get the lay of the land, see what might be cooking. You want to come along?"

He'd never hit her, except once when she was four years old. She'd never forgotten it, how she'd pulled away from his hand because she didn't need to have her hand held anymore, she was a big girl, and how ignoring his shout, "Susie! Susanna!" she had run, free, out into the crosswalk two beats after the light had changed. Horns, shouts, swearing, a breath of hot metal, and then three hard fast wallops on her bottom before being scooped up and crushed against his wildly beating heart. "Never," he'd said, his voice rasping in her ear, "never do that again, never." She never had, and neither had he.

"When are you going?" she said. Actually, it sounded kind of nice, the backseat, the window open, just looking at stuff, listening to their voices from the front but not really listening, just drifting, getting away, having everything peaceful and easy like it used to be.

"Right after breakfast. We've got an appointment to see one guy, a superintendent, head honcho, whatever, at ten-thirty. Then we thought we'd get some lunch; your mom remembers a place she used to go."

"Sorry," she said, finding, surprisingly, that she really was. She jiggled the tray. "Uncle Louie."

91

"Maybe Mike?" he started and then shook his head as she shook hers. "Guess not, no, guess you're stuck. Well, Mike'll be around if you need him. He wants to put in his hours on the garage. It's amazing what love'll do to a guy; he needs those bucks if he wants to spend half of every night on the phone. I'd better get dressed."

Uncle Louie wasn't up. The room was dim, the curtains she'd drawn over the French doors still shut, the stained glass facing the wrong way to get any morning sun. Susanna slid the tray onto the table, not sure what to do. He'd always been up before, sitting at his table or shuffling out from the bathroom. "Uncle Louie?" she whispered. "Are you awake?"

"Huh!" he said suddenly, and sat up, head shaking, arms flailing. "Huh! No. Get! Get away! No!"

"Uncle Louie, it's me. Susanna. Look." She hauled at one curtain then the other. Let him see her. "It's time for breakfast. You're probably hungry, right? It's morning."

His face was still twisted, frightened, but he slowly sank back. He raised one hand, trembling, too thin, and looked at it as though he'd never seen it before. He flexed it, closed it into a fist, and then let it drop down onto his chest. Then he turned his head away and closed his eyes.

"Uncle Louie?" What was the matter with him? Something twisted inside her. Was he mad at her this morning, mad because she'd been thinking about Melody so she hadn't been thinking about him, not *just* about him, and he knew it? Maybe, because yesterday afternoon, where had she been?

Not with him. And then last night he'd watched her sketching. She'd thought he'd like it, but he'd shown no interest in the three faces. He'd shut his eyes against them, slept.

It was too much, she thought suddenly. Worrying about both of them was too much. For one second she pictured water, clean and moving, heard voices weaving in and out, April laughing. "You don't have much to lose, do you?" Melody had said, but maybe Melody was wrong. Maybe she did have much to lose. "Yes," she said out loud, and it was almost a relief to say it, to have it over with, done with. Saying it sponged Melody's creek out, erased it, as though Uncle Louie's hand was guiding her own, because he knew that too much on a canvas clutters it. Wrecks it. Lines should be simple, clear, your own lines, not somebody else's, other people's who didn't even belong to you. Uncle Louie was her responsibility, not Melody. Melody had April. Uncle Louie didn't have anybody but her.

"Come on, Uncle Louie," she said now. "It's time to get up. Here, I'll help you, just sit up, that's right, that's the way." His hands were paper on bone, his feet, swinging free, were white and gnarled, like potbound roots. She'd seen her mother pull roots like that out, shake them to ready them for new dirt, a bigger pot. "Come on, Uncle Louie," she repeated.

He looked up at her, his eyes anxious again, then his hands gripped, he stood. "Will I be late?" he whispered. "He doesn't like it when I'm late."

"No," said Susanna. "No, it's okay, Uncle Louie. It's not late. Just, see, there's the bathroom, I'll get you some clothes, then I'd better heat this stuff up; it got cold."

"He doesn't like it when it's cold," Uncle Louie said. "I'd better hurry. Hurry." He shuffled into the bathroom, and with the door still open, started to pull down his pajamas.

"Wait," said Susanna, and fumbled the door shut. "I'll get you out some clothes," she said loudly. "You get dressed, okay, and I'll heat things up. I won't be long, okay?"

"Hurry," she heard him say, and then the toilet flushed.

Back out in the hall, hurrying, she found the tray was shaking, tea sloshing onto toast, juice into cereal. She'd have to do it all over, his whole breakfast, something was really wrong. It wasn't just Melody, but something more, something she must have done. Because he hadn't been like this the first day she'd seen him. When had that been? Friday? Only four days ago? Maybe she should tell her mother, but how could she if it was her fault, because she hadn't paid enough attention, because she'd done things too fast, maybe, or too loud, or too something.

Or maybe, she took a deep breath, a new thought, a good one, maybe this kind of thing just happened with old people: once in a while they had a bad dream, woke up confused. Probably it would just go away. When she went back with his new breakfast he'd be sitting washed and dressed at his table, and she'd help him eat. Her mother hadn't even told her that he'd need help eating. At least Susanna had noticed that, had done that right. She'd be all right, then, she'd handle it. Strong, her mother had said. The Grahame women were strong. She'd handle it.

"Are you sure you'll be okay?" Her mother was going out the door but stopped to watch as Susanna poured the reheated cereal carefully back into the bowl. "I feel bad, sweetie. I certainly hadn't meant for you to take over Uncle Louie completely. Don't think you have to give him your whole day, you know. He's used to being alone in his room; he likes it; it's the life he chose. His room *is* his life, that's what your grandma used to say."

It was almost funny. Don't give up, they said. Except Uncle Louie didn't seem to count. It was okay, it seemed, to give *him* up, to shrug your shoulders, let him go because he had chosen to live a way that was different. It was as though he wasn't even a person anymore. As though he was worthless.

"Anyway, Mike's out there working, if you need him, and there's money on the table. Why don't you get a pizza from Shirings for lunch? And Susanna, tomorrow, tomorrow you get the day off. I'll do Uncle Louie and you can do what you want to do. Okay?" She didn't see Susanna's face, was already turning away. "We'll be back around three, then. It's a nice day, try and get outside." Her voice drifted back through the screen door. She was down the steps, across the lawn. Susanna heard the car start up, pull out. They were gone.

The clock in the living room struck ten. Usually, Susanna stopped to listen: the ritual sixteen notes at the beginning of each hour so solid and satisfying, and then the pause before the count. Would it get it right, would it make a mistake this time? It never made a mistake.

But this time she hardly heard it. Outside, her mother had said. Susanna should have thought of that, outside. That's where her grandmother had taken him; Melody had seen them. He was probably missing them terribly, the sun, the warmth, the bench, but he hadn't known how to tell her. Yes. Probably the only thing wrong with Uncle Louie this morning was that he needed to be outside.

Chapter 13

He was dressed except for his socks. He was sitting at the table, looking down, he seemed to be, yes, Susanna's heart leapt, his hand was moving, he was drawing, he was fine! And then she saw that it was only his finger. He was bearing down hard with it, gouging an invisible pattern into the wood, mouthing something, his eyes intent. He didn't seem to notice as she set down the tray, stirred sugar into his tea, sprinkled it across the Cream of Wheat.

"Twenty." She heard him now, he was counting. "Twenty-one." His finger moved to the left, stopped, he frowned. "Twenty-two. Where's twenty-two?"

"Twenty-two what, Uncle Louie? Here's your cereal, time to eat your cereal."

He wasn't interested. "It's a ship, I can see that, but where? Where?" His hand raised suddenly, turned into a fist, swung at her. The bowl flicked out of her own hands, fell upside down on the floor. "Where did you put twenty-two?"

His face was working with rage, his fist swinging again, and Susanna backed away, cereal squishing underfoot. "Uncle Louie! Stop it!"

He sagged, bewildered now, and then, just as suddenly, looked frightened, cringed away. "Don't hit me," he said. "Please. Please, don't hit me." They stared at each other, both breathing rapidly, Susanna's heart thudding. Then, seeing her motionless, speechless, he slowly sank back and closed his eyes.

Susanna took a deep breath, let it out, looked down. The bowl was broken. The cereal had flown, splattered. She knew how it would dry, like concrete; she'd have to wipe it up fast, clean it up. She felt his bed against the back of her knees and, shaking, sat. Could she really have done this? Made him . . . crazy? Not funny crazy, *really* crazy?

He opened his eyes. "Tea?" he said.

"Tea?" Her voice shrill, parrotlike, she stumbled to her feet, picked up the spoon, moved the mug from the tray, and set it in front of him. Her hand was trembling, but his was, too. He slopped, then steadied, then drank. As she stood and watched him, he drank it all.

Then he stood up, scuffed barefoot through the remains of his cereal and opened the French doors onto the balcony. He hung for a moment on the threshold, lifting his face to the sky, and finally made his way slowly to his chair and lowered himself down. She heard him say something, and then again. "Outside," he said.

Right. Outside. He was outside, all right, outside, out of bounds, out of sight, out of it. Only minutes ago she had seen it, the picture in her head: she and Uncle Louie, walking hand in hand through the backyard, down the slope. Go slow, Uncle Louie, she'd been saying. Hold on, sit down now, look, the creek, the light, look at that branch over the water. The jet trails in the sky. The line of the bank, slanting over those bushes, under those jagged rocks. Look!

Right.

What had Melody said a few days ago? "That's a laugh, isn't it?" she'd said. Yeah, that was a laugh, Susanna thinking she could help Uncle Louie, get help from him. Her parents must be right after all, because her monkey tree was empty now. The monkeys sat huddled at its base, one on each side, alone, their paws over their eyes.

Susanna wiped her hand over own eyes. Right. Because she was back where she'd started, wasn't she? Where she'd been a week ago? Alone. And then she was shaking, she found she was shaking, and it was with anger, a clean cold wave of anger. She didn't know where it had come from, she'd never felt anything like it, but she *wanted* to feel it, it felt good, it felt *wonderful*. It felt wonderful to stomp into the bathroom, to kick away the pajamas that lay in a crumpled heap in front of the toilet, to grab the washcloth still hanging where she'd hung it the evening before. She ran the water until it was hot, soaked and wrung the cloth, and then stomped back out into the main room. Back and forth she went, wiping and rinsing, every trip stomping harder, sloshing harder, letting the anger build, feeding it, it felt enormous now, powerful, she could club somebody with it, she could *kill* somebody with it.

And then it turned on her, twisted, she could hardly breathe, and when she burst, finally, huddled on Uncle Louie's bed, her tears were like acid, hot and burning. All she wished was that they would melt her down, burn her away. But a few minutes later when she stopped crying she was still there. All that had melted was her anger, down to a hard little pebble deep inside. Every time she breathed she could feel it, yes, like a pebble, a pebble caught in a shoe.

It nudged her up, finally. Stony, yes, that was how she felt now, heavy, but cold, solid. She ran the tap again, cupping water up into her face again and again. Then she dried off, collected Uncle Louie's socks and shoes, and walked out onto the balcony.

"Uncle Louie." Not a question this time, but a statement, heavy, solid; not angry but cold, certain, *telling* him. She wouldn't frighten him, and he couldn't frighten her, not now. "I'm putting on your socks and shoes. Then we're going downstairs. Outside. I want us to go to the creek."

"No," he said, but faintly, only faintly, and after gazing at her as she pulled on his socks, he thrust his feet into his shoes and let her pull him up. She led him back into his room and then through it and then through his door to the hall. "No," he said again, but he didn't resist, he came. He stopped for a minute at the top of the stairs. "It's okay," she said. "There's the banister. Just hold on, one step at a time, I've got you. It's okay."

She let him rest on the half-landing, one hand firm on his, the other pointing through the window. "There's the garage, you remember the garage. And the swing? See, there's the swing."

"The swing?" He shook his hand free, and grasping the windowsill, pulled himself closer to look. "The swing," he said and his voice was different suddenly, firmer, as though a wave had been suddenly sucked back and the sand, free now from distortion, showed itself solid again, washed clean. "Sometimes she pushed, sometimes she stood over me, pumping, pumping both of us up, together. But I sanded the seats, painted them. Oak leaves once, acorns. I want to see them. I'll show you."

He was down two more stairs before Susanna caught up, grabbed his hand, steadied him the rest of the way. He shuffled eagerly across the kitchen, noticing nothing, until at the top of the back steps he stopped again and looked down at the hand holding his own. His eyes traveled up Susanna's arm to her face, and his own face crumbled back into confusion. And then fear. "*You're* not Mary," he said, trying to pull away. "Let me go!"

But the pebble hadn't softened. Susanna just grasped him more firmly, the words firm too; calm, she had never felt so calm, calm and cold. "It's okay, Uncle Louie, I'm Susanna, remember? It's okay. We have to go down to the creek."

"Do we?" he said and followed again, uncertain but no longer afraid—because I'm not, Susanna realized. Their slope did have stairs, a railing, and he went down, one step, then another, holding tight, a familiar journey, something he'd obviously done successfully, just like this, often before.

"It's not far," she said, "not far now." And it wasn't far, over a small rise and then another, and then they were there.

Chapter 14

By now Uncle Louie was breathing hard, sweat running down his face, down his arms, the hand holding Susanna's was wet. He couldn't have gone much farther than the bench, the bench she'd seen for the first time the day before. It was a green park bench, bought rather than built, its color glossy against the green of the scraggly bushes surrounding it.

"Here, Uncle Louie," she said, "sit down here." He followed obediently, but as she turned him to sit, he resisted, and with his free hand reached out and ran a finger over a small metal plate screwed to the wooden back. Something had been engraved on it in flowing, fancy script, and as she peered down to look, he read it for her.

"Mary's Bench," he whispered. "Mary's Bench." She looked at him, startled. There was something new in his face again, but this time his eyes, too, were different. They were smiling, *he* was smiling. "Mary's Bench," he repeated once more, nodding, and then turned and sank down as if coming home after a long journey. He unstuck his hand from hers to wipe it on his pants, and then, after a moment, unbelievably, slid it back. Still smiling, his breath quieting, his fingers grasping hers lightly, he shut his eyes.

Susanna sat, hardly breathing, and then slowly, slowly, as his hand continued, relaxed and trusting in hers, she felt herself melt. It's okay, she heard in her head, it's okay, and as she took a deep breath, sucking the warm air down, herself melting, the stone melting, she felt it was. It was as though for once, without really knowing how, she'd done something absolutely right. This minute, as the stone inside her dissolved to nothing, she didn't want to be anywhere else.

She could see why her grandfather had put the bench where he had. The creek here was down a steep bank, hard to get to, and it was narrower than behind Melody's, running deeper over its stones. It curved, curved again, changing constantly; you could watch it like a picture, but a picture that you could look at forever because, moving, shifting, it was always the same, always different. Beyond the creek, up the farther bank, was pastureland, at least she thought that's what they called it. She could see cows, and in the distance a silo and the roof of a barn. Some clumps of trees stood in just the right places; tall, a darker green, they lifted the eye. Every point, every line, was right. The fingers of her free hand flexed, like yesterday, wanting to draw.

Uncle Louie shifted beside her, tightened his hold. Yes, she'd been right to bring him here. Her grandmother, too, had known what a good place it was. When had they come? Had they waited each day until the car had pulled out, her grandfather off to school, until the chores were done, the morning chores of dishes and bed-making, hanging out a wash? Then, finally, the two of them, Mary, Louie, would have come out, out of his room, out of the house, come down here where nobody could stare at him or talk to him or scare him. They would have had good times down here, quietly, together. The best times, maybe.

Yes. The best times. But how many more would there be? *Lots* more, she told herself. *Lots*. If only she could shut off the picture she kept seeing in her head, a memory, a trip the fourth grade had taken at Christmas to sing carols at a nursing home. It had been terrible, sadder even than her mother's class, because the class, those kids, hurt as they were, were moving. Maybe only an inch at a time, but they were reaching, being pushed to reach, helped to reach because they could be. Maybe their up wasn't very high, but it was up. The nursing home, the faces, the smells, the bodies slumped, trapped in chairs, was no place but down.

Never, she thought. Never, Uncle Louie. Never.

But it wasn't something to worry about now. Now he sat peacefully where she had brought him. Free, if he wanted, to get up and go—well, she didn't know where, but wherever he wanted. Under his feet were grass and dirt. She should have thought of that. Gently untangling her fingers from his, she knelt down in front of him, slipped off his shoes, stripped off his socks.

Instinctively, his toes curled into the coarse grass. Then he raised both legs and wiggled his toes, letting his bare feet bask in the sun before dropping them back down. "Warm," he said, his eyes smiling again. Then they shifted to something over Susanna's right shoulder. They sharpened, and then his whole body shifted forward, tightening.

"What?" she said.

"Mary," he breathed, and then his face became radiant. "It's Mary," and he began struggling to his feet.

For a moment, Susanna refused to look. Whatever was there, or wasn't there, she didn't want to see it. But then she had to, because Uncle Louie, paying no attention to the weeds digging into his bare feet, had broken into a shambling run. She stood up, and then she saw, as he had, a small girl with dark hair, head down, wading along the edge of the water. It was April.

"Mary," he called, waving. "Mary!" April looked up, startled, and then, as though she too were seeing a ghost—or, in the old man flailing toward her, something much worse—her face filled with fear and she turned and began splashing back the way she'd come.

"Mary!" called Uncle Louie, his voice hoarse now with loss, and Susanna caught him just as he started over the bank.

"No," she said, grabbing for him, pulling him down, but

safe, into the weeds. He lay there, faceup, eyes stricken, and then he began to cry.

"Mary," he mourned. "Mary . . . Mary. . . ." Then, still crying, he closed his eyes and curled up into a tight ball.

"No, Uncle Louie," Susanna pleaded. "No, please, it's okay. It wasn't Mary, that girl, she's a girl down the road, her name is April. It wasn't Mary that left. I mean *now*. I mean, you've got her, you've always got her, in your head, inside you, she'll never leave you there, Uncle Louie. Uncle Louie, please."

But it was no good. His eyes closed tighter; he curled tighter. He didn't care that the hot noon sun was beating onto his head, that rocks and roots were burrowing into his side, that an ant was beginning to crawl up his bare ankle. She tried to take his hand, but it, too, was curled up hard, into a fist. "Uncle Louie," she said one more time. It was no good.

Help, she thought. I've got to get help. April? But April was too small, and Melody, she didn't know where Melody was. Who else was there?

Mike. For the first time in a long time she thought of her brother not with hurt or anger or confusion but with relief. Oh, thank God, Mike. Mike was strong. He could pick Uncle Louie up, carry him just like he'd carried her once, get him back into the house, into his room, safe. And he would. Maybe he couldn't help her anymore, but that wouldn't stop him from helping Uncle Louie. "Slide any farther down that hole . . ." her father had said, but he knew and she knew that Mike would come to the rescue of anybody who really needed him.

And then she was running, scrambling through the tall grass, panting, sweating, fast, because what if Uncle Louie uncurled, stood up, threw himself into the creek? No, she wouldn't think that, he couldn't, there were the stairs, up, up. When he was up, too, safe up in his room, she *would* tell her mother, tell her the second she stepped out of the car. Something's happened, she'd say, something's happened to Uncle Louie. Help him, please, because I can't. I thought I could, but I can't.

She was finally on the lawn, running across it. She could hardly see, her eyes blurred with sweat, but she could see the ladder; you couldn't miss the ladder angled against the back side of the garage. "Mike!" She tried to yell, but her breath was gone, gone, and he was looking away from her, reaching up under the eaves, the earphones of his Walkman plugged firmly into his ears.

"Mike!" It was stronger now, but he didn't hear, he still didn't hear her, see her. She put her hands on the ladder and she didn't shake it, she didn't mean to shake it. But then it suddenly shifted under her fingers, and Mike was sliding, falling, shouting, and then he and the ladder and the paint were lying in a silent tangle at her feet.

Chapter 15

"Melody! *Melody!*" The torn screen fluttered as Susanna pounded against the door frame, hammered with her knuckles and then with the palm of her hand. "Melody! Somebody! Oh, please, somebody come!" She had run all the way, and every word ripped at her throat.

And then the door slammed open toward her, scraping her arm even as she jumped back. A man loomed in the doorway, a stained T-shirt straining over his big gut, his face bleary, swollen, terrible, terrible, but she didn't care, couldn't care. "What the—" he started, but she grabbed onto him, interrupting.

"Please," she said. "My brother . . . please. . . ." A big dog thrust suddenly out from around the man's legs, and she froze.

He shook her hand off his arm, his stare incredulous. "You woke me up. You know that, don't you? Who the hell are you, anyway? What *is* this?"

Susanna squeezed shut her eyes so she wouldn't start screaming, because if she started she wouldn't stop.

"You're that kid from down the road, aren't you, that's been hanging around Mel? Mel's not here. April and her know enough to stay away and quiet when I say away and quiet. She'll hear about this. And you, you get out of here."

But instead of frightening her, every word he said stomped her panic down, until now it was the same cold nub of rage she'd felt earlier. There was no way she was going to leave until he helped her, and she didn't even care if he hit her. *She didn't care!* But he didn't hit her. Even as she answered him, her stare and her voice like ice, he blinked at her and, almost unbelievably, stepped back himself.

"I'll get out of here as soon as you tell me how to call an ambulance," she said. "My brother just fell off a ladder and broke something. I heard it snap. And my . . ." She stopped. She couldn't tell this man about Uncle Louie. "And my parents aren't home." He stared back at her for a long moment and then shook his head in disgust.

"Yeah, well, you should have said. . . ." He gave the screen another shove and jerked his chin at her. "Come on, then. Broke something, huh? Jesus. Listen, the problem is, yeah, I'll call the squad for you, but there isn't always somebody there.

They got trouble getting people during the day. They'll tell you to call the ambulance over in Alstair, but Jesus, that'd take an hour." He groaned, scratched at his stomach, sighed deeply.

"Listen, the best thing is just to load him up, take him right in. It'll have to be the truck, Lisa's got the car at work. What'd the kid break, you know? He conscious?" And then, a sudden bellow masking her reply. "Tom? Get on down here! *Now!*" He swung back to her. "What'd you say?"

"Yes," she repeated. And her voice was her own again, too, though it was shaking, she was shaking all over. She pushed at some stuff on a chair and sat down, scrunching her hands together tightly. It's okay, he's going to do something, it's okay. "For a minute I thought he was . . . was, but he was just kind of stunned. His head's okay, I think. It's his *leg*. Could you hurry, please?" She stumbled back up. "You know where it is? I've got to go back."

"Yeah, yeah, I got to get some clothes on. *Tom!* We'll be down; lucky the sleeping bags are still in the truck. Listen, tell you what. On your way out, you give that bell on that pine there a couple of pulls, that'll get those girls back up here from the creek. I'll send them on over. Who knows what the hell they can do, but Mel's as big as a Mack truck; maybe she can be some use for once. Jesus, what a way to start the day."

She still felt shaky, her legs precarious, like Popsicles melting on their sticks, ready to fall off. But she tottered toward the door, trying to hurry because she had to get back to Mike, now, right away. His face had been green under his tan, his eyes stunned, and she'd pulled the hammock down and piled it around him, because *don't move them*, she knew that, *cover them up, get help*. But to get help she'd had to leave him, leave Uncle Louie, and now her heart was thudding up into her throat. She couldn't breathe; she was going to be sick.

Suddenly something leaned against her knee, nudging at her, holding her up. It was the black, barrel-shaped dog, and he was grinning at her, his tongue and his tail busy, friendly. She groped for him and found his head bony and solid under her hand. "Good boy," she whispered, "good boy." He nodded at her, eyes happy. He took a step—you can do it—and then she could, one step, two, the sickness receding. He nosed open the door and led her out into clean noon heat. She took a deep breath, then another, only then realizing that the house had smelled, the air inside thick and sour like milk gone bad. Now she could breathe again, move again. What had he said, a bell, Melody? She ran toward the pine, the rope not a rope but two worn belts hooked together. She pulled them, then harder, and the bell spoke, clanked rather than rang, a large cowbell like in old movies about the Alps.

Two more pulls and then she was running again, the way she'd come, but this time she had company, the dog loping easily beside her. Mike was right where she'd left him, and his face blossomed in such naked relief when he saw her that her tears, held back so far, spilled up and over. She swabbed them away with one hand and with the other grabbed the dog's collar just as his tongue came out for a big lick.

"He won't hurt you," she panted. "He's friendly. Somebody's coming, Melody's dad, her brother, I think, they'll be right here with their truck." She sank down on her knees next to him. "Oh, Mike," she said and swabbed at her face again. "Mike, I'm sorry. I'm really sorry. Is it awful? Does it hurt really bad?"

"Yeah, but not so much if I lie still. But Susanna, it's my *leg*. You know, my *leg*. Training starts in two weeks. I'll never be on varsity now." He didn't even turn away as his own eyes filled and overflowed.

Susanna shut hers, pulling the dog tighter to her. "I'm sorry," she whispered. "I'm sorry."

"That *ladder*," he said. "You got a tissue? Yeah, well, it was that damn ladder. It's a piece of crap, it almost got away from me a couple of days ago, it doesn't sit right. Oh, man, I wish Dad was here. I wish . . ." He scrubbed at his face. "Listen, can you get this hammock off me? It feels like lead. I'm boiling."

He'd fallen in a tangle: ladder, Walkman, paintbrush, can, everything like a pile of pick-up sticks, and she'd agonized over how to get each one off without hurting him more. She'd slid and tugged at the paint-sticky ladder and finally he'd come free, groaning, his hand hovering helplessly over his leg, awful, awful. The hammock now was easy, just cloth. She bundled it up and away and the dog nosed at it, diverted momentarily from his two new humans.

"Mike, they'll be here soon, maybe the dog will stay, can

you grab his collar?" Her free hand was clenching, unclenching, she felt torn apart. "I've got to go down to the creek. Uncle Louie, I took Uncle Louie down there, and—"

"You're leaving me? Man, Susanna, these people coming, I don't know them, what do they know, people like that, they'll kill me. Man, please . . ."

"I've got to. I've got to. I'll be back as fast as I can. Don't let them take you. I'll be back, I'll go with you, Mike, I promise. But I've got to find Uncle Louie."

His eyes had turned to stone. His right arm came up to cover them but his left hand fumbled out and clamped onto the dog's collar as though it were a life ring. His mouth, too, clamped down, shut down, was silent.

She backed away and then turned and ran across the lawn, thrusting herself in leaps down the steps, kicking through bushes, her thighs burning, a cramp clenching up in her side, her breath rasping in and out like a dull saw catching and digging at bark. Rounding the tree-covered mound, she saw the bench, the clutter of socks and shoes, the unchanged landscape. But Uncle Louie was gone.

Chapter 16

When a few minutes later she hauled herself once again back up the steps, she saw that Mike was no longer alone. Melody was hunkered down next to him, April hovering behind, and a bright blue pickup was just pulling into the driveway. By the time Susanna plodded across the lawn, Melody's father had pushed his daughters aside and was staring avidly down.

"Jesus, you really did a job on yourself, kid," he said. "But, hey, you were lucky I was home, you're going to be okay. We'll have those doctors poking at you in no time. Okay, now, Mel, move your fat butt, we need those towels and those straps out of the truck. And grab that cot; April, you help your sister. We'll use it for a stretcher. We got to immobilize that leg, kid, anything going on with your back, you think? Your neck? Good. Then we'll just get that leg strapped up, pop you in the truck, we'll have you to the hospital in twenty minutes."

"Susanna!" April, en route to the truck, had eagerly detoured. "Susanna, listen, I've got to tell you. That old guy was down at the creek, did you know that? He was shouting something at me, I thought he was trying to get me. So I ran, but then I thought maybe he wasn't supposed to be there so I wanted to tell you. And your brother . . . Boy! What happened, Susanna? Tell us what happened!"

What happened? thought Susanna numbly. What happened was that she'd lost Uncle Louie. He was gone. She'd looked everywhere she could, stumbling around, calling his name, forcing herself for one terrible minute to peer over the bank, sure she'd see him splayed out, facedown in the water. But the creek was empty as far as she could see in both directions and it was too shallow to have swallowed him up. Which meant he was wandering somewhere, barefoot, confused. He could have fallen, too, broken something, too. What had she done?

"Hey, are you okay?" said Melody. "April, you climb over and hand that stuff down to me. Listen, Susanna, don't look like that, it'll be okay. My dad knows what he's doing, really, believe me, he likes all this first-aid stuff, he'd join the rescue squad but his schedule is so screwy because of his work. He does construction, when there is any. Here, grab these towels, okay? April, I've got the cot, just slide it out."

"Mel?" bellowed her father. "I didn't tell you to yap, lard-butt, I told you to *move!*"

Melody winced, and suddenly everything that had happened that day roiled up in Susanna's brain and exploded. She wheeled around, rigid with fury and yet shaking so hard that if she hadn't grabbed onto Melody's arm she would have fallen. *"What kind of a father are you?"* she screamed. *"Don't you know words can hurt people?"*

There was a moment of complete stillness. Nobody moved. Nobody spoke. And then Mike groaned. "Oh, man, Susanna," he said. "Oh, man . . ."

Melody's father nodded at him and kept on nodding. "Oh, yeah," he said. "You hurting, you needing help, and your own sister . . . Oh, yeah . . . *Oh*, yeah, a big mouth on that one." Then his chin jutted out. "Almost as *big* . . ." and he took two steps toward them, *"as my daughter's big butt!"* He let out a breath, and then another, and slowly unclenched his fists. He turned to his elder daughter. "Isn't that right, Mel?" he said softly.

Melody's face was a dull, splotchy red, but her voice was quiet. "Right, Dad," she said. "That's right."

"It's not right," Susanna said to her fiercely. "It's *not*."

Melody made an attempt at a grin, but her eyes suddenly were full of tears. Then she shook her head.

"Your brother," she said.

"That's right," her father said loudly. "Your brother. So, big mouth, you going to bring me those towels you're hanging on to or you going to let your brother lie here in the sun all day?"

Susanna looked down at the towels she hadn't even realized she was holding. Melody blinked hard and nodded. "It's okay," she said, and gave Susanna's arm a pat. Wordlessly, Susanna walked over and put them into the large outstretched hand.

"Right," he said once more, and then, turning away, concentrated all his attention on Mike, rolling the towels into bulky sausages and strapping them quickly but firmly around the hurt leg. Mike's mouth was still clamped shut, his face set but beaded with sweat, and he still clung tightly to the panting dog.

"You okay, kid? Now look, here's the cot, right? We'll start with your good side, just inch up onto it, slow now, no sudden moves, just slide up on there. I'll take care of the bad leg. Slow, slow. Ormil, get out of here. April, get that dog away, will you? Good, good. Now, Tom, you and Mel, take that end, I'll get this one. Jesus, the back of that truck's still up. April, you and big mouth there, yeah, *you*, what, you *deaf*? Show her what to do, April, yeah, okay, good. Now get out of the way."

Susanna got out of the way. Melody, breathing hard, her own face dripping with sweat, backed away from her father's impatient dismissal, and the two of them, with April, watched while Mike was carefully stowed into a corner of the pickup, packaged into a nest of camping gear and sleeping bags.

"Somebody's got to ride back here with him. You there, you think you can keep your yap shut long enough for that?" Susanna blinked. Ride with him. With Mike. Of course she wanted to ride with him. But she couldn't just leave without . . .

"Melody?"

Melody, beside her, seemed her old self again, brisk and competent. "You need to let your folks know, right? Well, April and I, we'll stick around until they get back, tell them where you've gone, okay? Ormil, get down from there, come on, now, you're staying with us."

"Thanks, but it isn't that, I mean it isn't *just* that. I mean, it's Uncle Louie. You know, April saw him down by the creek just now. I know he scared her, but he's not really scary. He's just old, he's all mixed up." She choked to a stop and then forged on. "See, it isn't just Mike. It's Uncle Louie, too. He's lost. I lost him."

"Hey!" from the truck. "Man, I can't believe you. We need to go *now*!"

"Please, oh please, just a minute, a second. . . . Listen, Melody. Can you find him? And then, please, just take him into the house, into his room upstairs, he'll know which one."

"Okay," said Melody's father. "I'm out of here. Tom. In back." The driver's door slammed, the engine started up and Susanna, who only just now noticed Tom, a tall, skinny boy with bad skin and hair like stubble, waved him frantically away and scrambled up into the truck herself. Melody shoved up the back and latched it.

"You can, can't you, Melody?" she said. "You will?" Now the passenger door slammed too, and the pickup lurched, reversed, and started backing out. Susanna grabbed for the side and then fell heavily onto her knees, hardly feeling the pain of scraping them over the gritty metal. "Please?"

"Hey!" Melody shouted as the truck lurched back into drive. She had Ormil firmly by the collar, and April, beside her, was waving hard. "Don't worry! I mean it. Don't worry about anything. I mean, what are friends for?"

What are friends for? Susanna sat down, scrabbling to find a good way to hold on. As the truck slowly picked up speed, she saw Melody's hand come up in a salute. Then Melody, April, and Ormil, the dog still struggling, still hoping for a ride, turned and started for the house.

The truck was moving faster now. Susanna felt her hair lift, her neck begin to dry and cool. Under her, the truck jounced, but only faintly. The road was paved, the ride surprisingly steady. Trees, fields, farms flowed past in a gentle stream.

Slowly, Melody's words echoing in her head, she felt herself relax into the one good thing she could take out of this nightmare of a day. Why had she screamed at Melody's father?

Partly because of . . . everything, but partly because he was hurting someone she hadn't even realized had become a friend. It hadn't helped at all, but that's why she had done it, and Melody knew that. She had tried to help Melody, and now Melody would try to help her. Friends.

Everything else . . . Uncle Louie still hunkered painfully inside her, hurt maybe in a way that maybe nobody could fix. And Mike . . .

She'd scraped her knees raw, but she was glad of the punishment as she crawled back over the dirty corrugated metal to where he sat, carefully propped against the back of the cab. His eyes were shut, his mouth slightly open, his head slumped against a heavy roll of sleeping bag wedged into the corner. She hunched down beside him and took his hand.

He started, looked at her wildly, just like Uncle Louie earlier: Who are you, stay away, get away! Please Mike, she thought, please, what are friends for, and felt her tears spring up again. I'm sorry. I'm sorry. His mouth turned down, quivered, and then his eyes closed again, but bending over him she could see that it was only to keep his own tears in. She wiped away the one that escaped and reached again for his hand. And then his own fingers took hold, too, clamping down, as earlier they'd clamped onto the collar of the dog.

If she could only give him that much comfort. The thought calmed her as she settled down beside him as close as she could get. It had been a long time since they'd been able to give each other as much as that. And if she could do that—and she would if it killed her—a part of her wished that the ride to the hospital would never end.

Chapter
17

He's going to be all right." Susanna's mother dropped down onto one of the molded plastic chairs that lined the waiting room and pushed the hair off her face. Her husband was having one last word with the young doctor who stood propped, half in and half out of the swinging door that led to wherever it was that they did whatever they did. They hadn't let Susanna in. Nobody had even spoken to her for the three and a half hours she'd waited for her parents, except a frizzy-haired nurse who'd been annoyed that Susanna hadn't known a whole series of critical details about insurance.

"He might have a slight concussion, though, so they're going to keep him in overnight, just for observation." Now it was her father's turn to sit, heavily; the chair skittered, complained. It was cracking up the back, and Susanna had counted, over and over, the fourteen cigarette burns tattooed in a neat triangular pattern on the seat. They looked old, but then everything about the waiting room looked old except for the shiny NO SMOKING sign over the front door. "But the break looks clean—the fibula, the doc said, and simple, not compound. Mike was lucky. And I guess whoever brought him in while we were wasting our time with school officials did a good job of immobilization. A neighbor, he thought? What happened, Susanna?"

That's what everybody wanted to know. What happened? And that was important, yes. But the question about Mike that had been reverberating louder and louder as the afternoon had worn on wasn't "What happened?" at all. It was "What about football?"

How could he be okay if, when his team trotted out onto the field that bright September afternoon, he wasn't there? It wasn't pain that had caused those tears to ooze out of him earlier, but everything the pain meant, the way it slobbered great gobs of black paint over his picture of who he was, of the place that he held in his life. So how could they all leave him there, overnight, alone, with nothing to do but stare at the ruins of his junior year? She felt again the clutch of his fingers around her hand, and stood up.

"Hey, babe," said her father, and standing himself, eased her back down. "You don't look so good either."

"Susanna?" said her mother, her arm tight around her. "It's all right, sweetie. He's going to be all right. And *you* did just right, getting help. Why did we have to pick today to talk to that idiot of a superintendent, but *you* did fine, coming with him, sitting here all this time. You must be exhausted. And hungry. I'll bet you didn't get any lunch, you must be starved."

Why is it worse when they say nice things and they're wrong? When they don't see you, see what you really are, just see what they want, what they hope. And you can't tell them, you can't because it would crush them, the truth, and you'd never get the wrinkles out, it would never be smooth again, their love, it would never feel right again, they would never feel the same.

"Come on, Susie," said her father. "Let's get you home. I think I saw a hamburger joint coming in. We'll stop and get you something."

"I need to see Mike." She couldn't fix what had happened, but at least she could let him see that she *knew* what she'd done. *Understood* what it meant. "Please, just for a minute." She saw them exchange a glance and then her father sighed.

"Room one-fifty-eight. Let me—"

"I can find it." Rude again, but she had to go alone.

"Let me tell the nurse here," her father finished gently. "It's just down that hall. But, Susanna . . ." She steadied herself against the front desk. She *was* dizzy. She hadn't realized how hungry she was. "He's pretty tired. Don't stay long."

He was in the bed near the window, a blanket folded neatly away from the white cast that turned his whole right leg into something bloated, inhuman, clamped onto him against his will. His face was still speckled with white paint, and his eyes, when he turned to her, looked less groggy than puzzled. Of course. He, most of all, would want to know. How had all this happened?

Uncle Louie crawled into her head as he'd been doing all afternoon, crawled in, looked at her, crawled back out. Every time, she slammed the door against him, but it never latched. He always got back in. Maybe explaining would quiet him, too. Give him some rest. Give them both some rest.

"Mike, listen. I took Uncle Louie down to the creek and even though I think he liked it, I shouldn't have. I didn't know what I was doing. And something upset him, he wouldn't come back up again. He lay down, he wouldn't even *get* up again. So I came to get you, to help him, help me. But you couldn't hear me. So I . . . I put my hand on the ladder, I didn't mean to shake it, but I think I did. I think I must have. So it's all my fault. About football, everything . . . All my fault."

But he still looked more puzzled than anything else. "I didn't see you. I don't remember anything moving. I just remember reaching, you know, I was doing the overhang. That ladder wasn't long enough. I don't think it was you. I don't blame *you*." Then his mouth twitched and he gave her a look she hadn't seen for so long, that older brother "you're such a brat" look that she'd hated and missed so much.

"Well, I mean, except for maybe your big mouth. I didn't think you had it in you anymore, sounding off like that. Man, was he mad. What a weird guy. Except he got me here okay, he knew his stuff." Then he gave a long, shuddering sigh. "Oh, man. It's just all so dumb, all of it. So dumb. I wasn't even that high. . . ."

He didn't blame her, then. She could breathe again. And again, she saw him fall, as she'd been seeing him in her mind all afternoon. "I think you got twisted," she said, slowly. "Like you were trying to hook your foot around the ladder to hold on. Like . . ." Like a monkey, she thought. Were there three monkeys in that tree, then? At least. Oh, at least. But there was something else she wanted to say, something that might really help. "Mike, do you want me to call Kim? She could phone you here."

He tried to sit up. "No way. No way she's going to know." His voice now was rough, as twisted as his foot around the wood that had snapped his leg. Now it was her turn to look puzzled. "Man, you don't get it, do you? Why do you think I've been calling her every night we've been here, every day? With me away, they're lining up, Colletti, Robertson, all those guys. They're all dying to move in, ask her out, they're just waiting for a chance like this. That's all I got going for me, football. I'm nothing without it, nothing. I never could do stuff like you and Dad, art, music. . . . With me off the team, you think Kim'll even look at me? Somebody like her, she could have anybody, college guys, anybody."

Susanna had never seen a more terrible look on anyone's face. Even Uncle Louie hadn't shown this naked pain, because Mary, his Mary, might be gone but she'd loved him, he knew that, was sure of that with every cell in his body. But Mike . . .

could he really think that? Kim, the girl he'd spent every free minute with for over a year, all those dances, flowers, that gold chain he'd bought her for Christmas and was still paying for. . . . Could he really believe that she was just using him? That he was just a football away from nothing?

Susanna found herself shivering, understanding finally what he'd tried to tell her the day before, that it wasn't dislike he'd felt for her at all, but fear, fear that he could just as easily end up just as lost. And if *Mike* could feel like that, *Mike*, well, then, couldn't everybody?

But this wasn't the time to think about everybody. "You're *not* nothing," she said fiercely. "And it's *not* just football. Oh, sure, you're good at football, you're *great* at football, but you're good at everything, don't you know that? And Kim loves you, I'm sure she does, but if she's dumb enough not to, well, don't you know that half the girls in your class would practically kill to take her place? And . . ."

Mike was staring at her, his mouth open, but at least that terrible look was gone. "Okay," he was saying, "it's okay, Suz"—he was actually patting her arm—"thanks, it's okay." But then his eyes hardened again and his hand tightened. "But you've got to promise me," he said. "Promise me you won't call her; Mom either; promise me, Suz, I need you to. Please," he said. This time he said it out loud, "please," and she couldn't remember why she'd ever wanted to get back at him. All she wanted now was to wipe that look from his eyes, let him begin to mend in some kind of peace.

"I promise," she said, and then she looked at him and said it again. "I promise." He clutched her arm for one more second and then nodded and slumped back against his pillow.

"Okay," he said.

"We'll be back in the morning."

"Okay," he said again, and sighed. Then, his eyes still shut, his mouth twitched again into a kind of smile. "Hey. You know what? There's one good thing, anyway. At least now I don't have to finish painting that damned, stupid, ugly garage."

Chapter
18

"Oh, Susanna, here. I almost forgot."

Susanna was in the backseat with a half-eaten hamburger dumped back in its bag. She'd thought she'd been hungry, but the bun was like cotton, those thick wads they stick in with vitamins. The car was going too fast, but not fast enough; she wanted to be home right *now*, but never. What would be there, waiting? Or not waiting. Mike was at least safe now, looked after, the hospital room a neat white package she could safely close him into overnight, open him up from tomorrow. Home, though, was a jungle, one of those nightmare ones, horrible things dropping out of trees, traps opening underfoot at every step. . . . She blinked. "Huh?" she said, staring at the envelope in her mom's hand.

"*You* are going to bed early, that's all I can say. I think we'll all probably go to bed early tonight. *Here.* That girl, Melody, it was nice of her to wait and tell us about Mike. Her sister's so tiny, isn't she? Melody's so huge. Neither of them could be eating right. It's a shame, they could be pretty girls."

Susanna wasn't listening. Melody had sent her a note. A letter, really, with one of those envelopes you can make by folding a piece of paper just right. Susanna swallowed. The hamburger wasn't cotton anymore but dirt, heavy and getting heavier as it expanded in her gut. What was that myth they'd read in the fourth grade, that girl Pandora who opened that box and everything bad in the world flew out and could never be stuffed back in, never?

But not opening it would be worse. It would be better to know now about Uncle Louie, and then if she had to she could tell her father to stop the car and she could be sick and then she could run and run, except the fields here were corn, too tall to run through, not tall enough yet to hide in.

Slowly she fumbled open the paper. At first she didn't see any writing at all, just a picture, a snapshot of somebody she didn't even know, a woman, not too old, heavy, with dark heavy hair. Then she saw that the envelope was the letter, too, one side with just her name, the other covered with handwriting like you see in books, every letter perfectly formed, perfectly connected to the next.

"Hi. This is my Mom, in case you still want it, but I need it back. Can you come over tomorrow? I told you not to worry. He was right up there, in his room. That place is really something, isn't it? Anyway, he seemed to just want some water and so we gave him some and put him to bed. That's what he wanted. I hope that was okay. Call me when you get back. And Susanna, thanks, I . . ."

But Susanna was crying too hard now to read the rest. He wasn't dead, then, she hadn't killed him, he was okay. It was too much. . . . She hardly felt the car slow, pull over, hardly heard the car door open, close, open again, but when her mother slid beside her and took her in her arms, every inch of her was so astonishingly solid and real, so astonishingly safe and right, that Susanna grabbed on, held on, never wanted to let go ever again.

But she did, finally. She sat up finally, slowly, and she saw that her mother was crying, too, and then her hand was smoothing down over Susanna's face over and over. "Tell me, Susanna. Whatever it is, you can tell me. You can always tell me."

So Susanna told her. Told them both, because her father was gripping the back of the seat so hard his fingers were white, his face all angles, like when he'd run into the hospital. "Where's Mike?" he'd said then, but now it was for her, so she told him, too.

It came out in a jumble: monkeys, practice, Uncle Louie who could save her and be saved, the creek, the ladder, the pile of shoes and socks that jarred the rest of the world into emptiness because they told her Uncle Louie was gone. Melody came out, Melody's father, Mike. Mike. And, finally, again, Uncle Louie, because of all the things wrong he was the worst, had been damaged the most. What had she done to Uncle Louie?

"Whoa," said her father. "Whoa, now." And Susanna stopped, let her mother mop her face, and then took the tissue from her and blew her nose. "If I've got this right, Susie, what you're saying is that Uncle Louie is losing it, fast. Uncle Louie, Uncle Louie, I know *nothing* about Uncle Louie. Meggie, how was he when you came? Or the last time you took food to him, last week, how was he then?"

"Oh, Susanna." Her mother rummaged in her purse for another tissue and blew her nose, too. "This is all my fault. You tried to ask, but I didn't tell you, at least didn't tell you right. It's just that . . . Listen, did you hear what your dad said? Losing it. Well, twenty years ago, Uncle Louie brought all those beautiful things into that room and just . . . lost it. He stopped. Everything about him . . . stopped, because that's what happens. If you're so afraid you'll be hurt that you just close yourself up, you . . . you *die*. Life is *hard*, but it's *life*. It can be scary, it can be terrible, but it's all the wonderful things, too: love and friendship and work, wonderful things he just gave up."

"No." Susanna had to break in. Her mother was wrong. "Uncle Louie loved Grandma," she said. "And work, his art. He had his art. His room . . ."

"Did he?" said her mother. "He loved Grandma, but did he ever see her, see her the way she really was? A woman who was getting old? Who was tired? Who had a bad heart? I don't think he did, Susanna. And his art? What art? He never did any art in that room. Grandma told me that once, she was so sad about it, she thought she'd failed him, but it wasn't her. It was him. Art's like life, it's hard, it's risky, he couldn't do it. Sure, the room was beautiful, *is* beautiful, yes. But is that *enough?* Even if it was enough for him, is it *enough?*"

"Meggie," said her husband.

She shuddered to a halt. "I'm sorry," she said. She sighed and clasped her fingers in her lap. "I'm sorry. You weren't asking about all that, were you? You need to know how Uncle Louie was last week. The truth is, and it's terrible, I didn't really notice. He was always sitting there when I went in, always dressed, certainly. Maybe, now that I'm thinking about it, he was never *un*dressed, maybe it was always the same clothes, there *was* a kind of smell. And he didn't say much. I'm trying to think if he said anything, but as I keep trying to tell you, Uncle Louie wasn't up in that room to talk to people. I guess what I'm saying is that I didn't expect anything from him, so I wasn't surprised when I didn't get it."

"But he talked to me," said Susanna stubbornly. "At least, a little. About Grandma, about when they were kids."

"And that's *good*, Susie," said her father. "You did him good. But this 'when they were kids,' that's a clue. What your mother is saying is that Uncle Louie started this retreat a long time ago. It's like he's been running backward for years and now he's almost there, back where he was little, safe. I don't know, this is getting a bit murky, but, maybe, now he's running even faster. The thing is, it wasn't *you*, Susanna."

"Yes, of course it wasn't, but from what Susanna said, it's

more than that, it's physical decline now, too, taking care of himself, washing." His wife shook her head. "If he's started down *that* incline, that quickly . . ."

"Whoa," said her husband again. "We don't know that, Meggie. We don't know much of anything, really. I think what we've got to do now is get on back to your father's house and find out what's really going on with Uncle Louie."

Chapter 19

Uncle Louie was asleep. At least when Susanna had left him an hour before he had been asleep, lying like a carefully placed rag doll under his light blanket, his eyes obediently closed, his breathing light and steady. Her parents were in bed, too. Like her father had said, it had been quite a day, and tomorrow would probably be more of the same. They'd probably all better get as much rest as they could. If the phone rang again, let it ring. Unplug it, even. Throw it in the creek. Enough, already. Sleep.

But Susanna couldn't. Partly, it was just too hot. Her room, for the first time, choked her, with its one small window that earlier in the summer had been pounded open as high as it would go. Moths squeezed in around the old screen, mosquitoes, but the air stayed out, stayed stuck. Stuck, sticky, itchy. Her mind stuck, too, then jerked, jerked her awake, jerked her finally up, out, down the stairs, trying not to creak. Maybe it would be better on the porch.

It was. She sat in a rustle of night sounds, the glider snicking back and forth, the canvas covers tight and cool after the hot rumple of her bed. Breathe, she could breathe here. Her thoughts could slow; she could count them over, set them down, maybe they'd stay, form a pattern that could rest until morning.

The calls earlier had formed a pattern. Most of them, of course, had been about Uncle Louie. Susanna could hardly believe that a week ago she hadn't even known Uncle Louie; and then she'd felt she'd known him in a way she'd never known anybody before, and now they were going to take him away. She'd opened his door this afternoon and seen his eyes and then the smell had hit her, hit them all. She'd carried the soiled clothes down to the laundry room and helped her father remake the bed while her mother got Uncle Louie into a bath and out again. Their voices, their gestures, had been gentle, patient, and Uncle Louie had slowly quieted, had drunk some tea, eaten some cereal. He hadn't seemed to notice that the hands rubbing antiseptic cream into the scrapes on his feet were male hands, the kneeling figure a man, and a man he'd never seen before. He didn't seem afraid. Just confused and very, very tired.

But that was here. Here he could handle. Whatever strange

things were happening in his head, at least they were happening in his room, filled with his chosen things, peopled by his ghosts. But they weren't going to let him stay. Susanna could tell from the bits she'd heard of conversations with doctors and public health nurses and nursing homes that what her mother was looking for was a place, a bed, somewhere else, away. Can't he stay here, she'd asked, she'd cried, but this time her mother hadn't hugged her, held her, comforted her. "How?" she'd said. "Who? Me? You? Your grandfather? Uncle Louie's full time, now, Susanna. That's more than any of us can give."

And the worst thing was, she was right. Susanna curled herself tighter on the glider and rocked, rocked. She should be willing to go up there every day and do everything that had to be done. She wasn't a baby anymore. But Uncle Louie was, or would be, and she couldn't, she just couldn't. So they'd take him away, terrify him with strange hands and faces, strange rooms and smells. She could hardly stand it, thinking about it, but he'd have to do it, he'd have to stand it, the torture of it, the torture. . . .

Stop it! She wrenched herself up and started pacing, slapping her bare feet against the coarse straw matting covering the porch floor. Remember what Grandpa said, this evening on the phone. Remember.

It had been the last call before Susanna's father had gently pulled his wife away from the phone and sent her to bed. "He wants to talk to you," she said to Susanna as she went. "It's

Grandpa. He's flying back tomorrow. I've got his flight number but I forgot to ask him the time. Can you . . . ?"

Susanna had picked up the phone. "Hello?"

"Hello, Susanna? I won't keep you. Sounds like you've all had a day. Sounds like it was high time I was back there to give you a hand. Susanna, your mom just told me about Louie, and I just wanted to tell you that I don't want you to fret about this. Louie, well, this has been coming for some time, not that I had any idea it would come this far this soon. But I don't want you thinking for one minute it was you, honey. Of course it wasn't. Louie, well to me, Louie was a goner from the minute he walked into that room. Except . . . you still there?"

"Yes. But . . . well . . . except what?"

Her grandfather had sighed. "I didn't like Louie. I'm sorry to say that, but it's the truth. I didn't and I don't. But thinking about it, and I've thought about it a lot the last few days, I have to hand him one thing. He shut himself up from anything *I'd* ever call a life, but—and here's the 'except'—it was what he wanted. Not many people get to spend twenty years of their life living exactly how they want. So I guess I have to admire him for that. That . . ." his voice had cracked, "that and the fact that your grandmother loved him."

Susanna broke in, just as she had with her mother earlier. They had to understand. "He loved her, too, Grandpa. He . . . he still does. It's because she's gone, I think, that he . . ." She had to stop to swab at the hot tears falling all over her hand.

"Yes," he'd said finally. "I think so, too. Well, I'm coming home tomorrow, honey. I can't take care of him like . . . she did. I just can't. But he's got money, Louie does, and I'll make sure he's in a good place, a *kind* place."

"Could he have some of his things?" Somehow that helped the most, the thought that not everything would be ripped away. His pictures, maybe. His chair. The small curve of fox he could cradle in his hands.

"I don't know why not. Maybe you could help me pick what you think would comfort him the most before you head on home. Your mom says you probably *will* go, says the money they're paying teachers here is pitiful, ain't *that* the truth. But speaking of going, one other thing, although we can talk about it more when I get there. Four-forty, did I tell your mother that? Four-forty. Yes, well, especially as it looks like I've decided not to retire right away after all, do you think you might consider coming back for a visit? Next summer, maybe? I'd just . . . well, I'd like the time to finally get to know you—you and Mike. How does that sound?"

It had sounded fine. But now there was another sound, something was ringing, and Susanna jolted back from her grandfather's comforting words and registered what it was. The phone. Unplug it, her father had said, but of course they hadn't, what if the hospital needed to call, what if Mike . . . ? The living room, the kitchen were dark, but she knew the way now, the old black receiver so heavy she almost dropped it. "Hello?" She was gasping for breath, tried again. "Hello?"

"Susanna? Is that you? I'm sorry to call so late. It's Kim. Mike usually calls me, but I was out baby-sitting. These neighbors phoned me after supper so I went, spur of the moment. Never again, those kids were terrible. But is Mike there? Can I talk to him?"

"Promise me," he'd said, and she'd promised, but what to say, how not to lie? "There's lots of ways to lie," her father had said, "and I don't like any of them," and she didn't either. But between a promise and a lie, what do you do when nothing you *can* do is right?

"Susanna?"

"I . . . I think he's asleep." He probably was, she hoped he was. "He had a kind of a rough day. Can he call you tomorrow?" Tomorrow Mike would be home. Tomorrow he could find out how much was broken along with his leg.

"I'm baby-sitting again tomorrow," said Kim. "Can I give you the number? Let me give you the number, I don't think he has it. We're going to their cottage for a couple of days." Susanna heard a rustle of paper, a sigh; she, too, scrabbled for a pencil, wrote the number down. Kim sighed again. "What a summer," she said. "I'm supposed to be making all this money, but it's all for college, I don't even see it. These kids are really getting to me, and Mike's away. I really miss him, Susanna, you know?" Her voice was soft now, near tears. "Well, maybe not, he's your brother, but I do, he's such a special guy, believe me, so many of the guys around here are such jerks. But Mike, well, he's not. . . . I just wish you'd come back home. When are you coming back home?"

"Kim?" If Susanna heard much more she'd cry, too, she knew she would, and then she'd tell Kim everything, and it was Mike who should hear this, hear that he was wrong. Kim's voice and words said he was. "Kim. You tell him, okay? Tomorrow, you tell him, he'll really want to talk to you, he just can't now. I've got to go. But he'll call you, okay? He will." She hung up.

The weight had shifted a little, lifted. It was funny what would help, who would, people you didn't expect: Melody yesterday, her grandfather, now Kim. Even Melody's father earlier. She could never like him, but even people like that sometimes helped you, made things easier. Easier, but then harder to shut out. Once they help you, you help them, you can't ever really shut them out again. The funniest thing of all is that then, finally, you don't even want to anymore.

Chapter 20

It wasn't so bad at first. When Susanna carried the tray into Uncle Louie's room the next morning, he was up, not dressed, but he'd used the bathroom, he seemed rested, calm at least, more like he'd been a few days back. He ate something, drank something, he got all his clothes on without help except his socks and shoes. Even his feet looked better, just a few scraped places, a few bruises. He headed toward the balcony, then, moving quickly, eager, it seemed, to get to his chair, say hello to his spider, settle into his familiar view of trees and sky. When she took his hand, instead, turned him, he looked puzzled at first, and then frowned. "No," he said and shook her hand away.

"Come on, Uncle Louie," said Susanna's father from the doorway. "Come on, now, it will be okay," but it wasn't, it wasn't at all. Susanna wished she could run, but her father felt the same way, she could see he did, so she reached again gently for Uncle Louie's hand, and this time he didn't shake it off. He clung to it as step by painful step they urged him down the stairs, through the kitchen, out of the house. Not fair, she thought, three against one, not fair, and she was almost glad when he refused to get into the car. She was almost proud of him.

But then they were too strong for him—of course they were too strong, he was just a frail old man—and he was crouched into a ball in the backseat and Susanna's hand felt all bone, gripped so hard that any moment it might crack, break, splinter into fragments that would mix with his own.

"I'm here, Uncle Louie," she whispered. "And Mary's here. She'll never leave you, she won't, think about Mary, Uncle Louie, and the swing and the cereal and playing in the sand." He relaxed, just a little, so over and over she said it, over and over, all the way to the hospital and the wheelchair they had ready and all the way into the office, when she had to stop, because the doctor took him and he was gone. Finally the doctor reappeared.

"His blood pressure's sky high," she said. "And he's dehydrated and, of course, obviously, disoriented. I'd like to admit him for a few days, then we'll see. . . ." She noticed the look on Susanna's face and continued gently. "Try not to worry.

Once he's settled, he'll be fine. Fine." But he wouldn't be, Susanna knew. He was lost, they were leaving him. He was gone.

"We'll come back tonight, Susanna, I promise you," said her mother. "We'll come back and see him, make sure he's all right. Oh, sweetie, I know it's hard, I don't know why so many things are just so hard. I wish I could help you more with this. I wish I could help you more." And just having her say that, just pocketed between them, her parents, in the front seat as Mike struggled to make himself comfortable in the back, just having Mike there, okay, himself, all of them there, together, it did help. The weight, so heavy again this morning that she thought it might crush her, lifted, as it had last night, just enough.

It lifted a little more when, as they turned into the driveway, she saw Melody sitting on the steps. It was amazing how Melody knew when she was needed, even when you hadn't known it yourself.

She heard a sigh from the backseat. "Do me a favor?" said Mike. "You know, thank her for me, her dad? I just can't face it right now."

Susanna wiggled around so she could see her brother's half-averted face. Kim. She hadn't told him.

"Kim," she said. "I'm sorry. I forgot. She called last night."

"Kim called? She called *me*? What did you say?"

Susanna twisted just enough further that she could look into his face. "I said you were asleep. She left some new number. I said you'd call her back today." Then she couldn't help it, it felt so familiar and comfortable to be just a little mean. "Don't you want to know what *she* said?" The look in his eyes was enough of an answer, and mean was silly, not what she wanted at all. She undid her seat belt and, kneeling, leaned between the headrests so that only he could hear. "She said all the other guys are jerks. She said she missed you. She said . . ."

"Oh, man," he said, and he was struggling to get the door open, struggling to get his crutches under him, and then they were all out, and Susanna saw the ladder and remembered the room upstairs, the empty room, and if it hadn't been for Melody planted in front of her, the weight of it all would have come right back down on her all over again.

Melody, as usual, wouldn't let it. "Let's go sit on your screened porch, okay?" she said, smiling politely at Susanna's parents, but nudging Susanna gently toward the back of the house. When they were safely out of earshot, she stopped, but she kept her voice low. "Listen, I partly came over to tell you that your brother saved our lives. Dad loves doing stuff like that, he's still feeling good, and after that camping trip we figured it would be weeks."

She hesitated, glancing at Susanna, then away. "See, you've got to understand how he is. I know he sounds bad. Talk about a big mouth, where does he think *I* got it? But that's usually all it is, you know, bad-mouthing. I don't want you to think, well, *you* know. Only once, and, well, I was mouthing off, too, and yeah, he clobbered me one, and well, hey, I clobbered him back and headed down here until I cooled off, he cooled off, and then I wouldn't go back until I told him what Mom told *me*." She pulled open the door to the porch, squeezed in and collapsed onto the glider. "She kind of had to say it all before she died, you know, even the stuff she probably wouldn't have told me until now, about guys, stuff like that."

"Like . . . what?" said Susanna, sitting beside her and starting to rock. Her own mother wasn't very good at talking about that kind of thing, not that she'd ever asked. Maybe it was time she did. Maybe that's what her mother had been trying to tell her, that she was just waiting for her to ask.

"Like, if a guy ever hits you, *ever*, for *anything*, you get out fast and never, you never go back. I figured that meant fathers, too. Why not?"

Susanna nodded. That made sense to her. "What did he say?"

"He said he was sorry," said Melody. "But *I* said sorry wasn't enough and if he ever hit me again, or April, we were out of there. We'd go to my aunt's and we'd tell everybody why. Well, he heard me okay. And he knows I'd do it. He knows me pretty good." She sighed. "But he does have a bad mouth, especially when he's laid-off. He hates that. He's only this bad, really, when he's not working, and even Lisa was laying low this time, and usually she can handle him pretty good. But this thing with your brother yesterday, and then this morning the union hall called, well, I tell you, things are looking up." She nodded, settling herself more comfortably into the corner of the glider. "So how about *you?*"

Susanna was still a few sentences back. "But it isn't just hitting, Melody. It *isn't*. Words hurt, too, almost as bad. Don't guys, people, have to hear that, too, that they shouldn't. . . ."

Melody grinned. "Well, Dad sure heard it from you yesterday. That took a lot of guts. I don't know if he got the message, but it's funny, I thought he'd yell at me after and he didn't, really. He just said you sure take after your gran, don't you? Of course, I have to tell you, he didn't much like your gran. See, she said that, too, that time. She went back to my place with me that morning and she told him how yelling was almost as bad as hitting and he shouldn't be doing either one."

"Well, he shouldn't," Susanna repeated stubbornly.

Melody nodded again. "Yeah, okay, he shouldn't. But so . . . ? It sounds like it means something to you, this yelling stuff."

"So," Susanna said slowly. "So, yes. That's what happened. To me. Nobody hit me, it wasn't that, it wasn't even guys." She took a deep breath and let it out. "It was this girl. Amanda. She was my best friend. My best friend, and then she wasn't, but I didn't know it. I kept telling myself she was just busy. That's what she'd say every time I called, that she was busy. 'We've got to start planning for Artfest,' I kept saying, but she always had some excuse, something else she said she had to do." And now the words were tumbling out as fast as she could say them.

"Well, I should have known something was wrong, then. I mean Artfest, it's this arts competition we'd always entered together every spring, Amanda and our other friend Megan, before she moved, and me. *Always*, since the third grade. And

147

I had a great idea this year, a mural with puppets people could move to make funny scenes, and I knew Amanda would love it, it was just her kind of thing. But it was getting late; I just couldn't understand why she didn't want to get started on it. She knew we had to get started if we wanted to win."

Susanna stopped and laced her shaking fingers together to keep them still. The glider snicked back and forth, back and forth, and she took another deep breath and went on.

"So I stopped her in the hall one day. She was with this group of girls I hardly knew, I thought *she* hardly knew, and I said, 'Amanda,' I said, 'there's only a month till Artfest, come over Saturday, okay?' And then . . . and then, in front of all these other girls, and I could see now she did know them, they were all smirking, she just started screaming, I don't know why, I've never known why, screaming so that everybody in the hall could hear about how babyish I was to still like art, and how she was tired of me bugging her about it. Because any day I wouldn't be able to do it anymore, didn't I know that, because that's what had happened to her. And she was *glad* it had happened because she hated art now, didn't I know it meant nothing to her—it was boring and stupid and any-body who still liked it was boring and stupid too, just like me. So I should leave her alone, just leave her alone." She stopped, staring down at her hands that were clasped so hard that the ends of her fingers showed dull red under the white of her knuckles.

"So?" said Melody again.

"Why do you keep saying that, so? So it was a curse. A curse, because I *am* boring and then I *couldn't* do it anymore, art, at least not any good anymore. That's what my teacher said. My *art* teacher. At the end of my most important year. Because you have to show your portfolio, you know, to get into the real art classes in high school, the art classes where you really learn something. So my art teacher took one look at my final project, and she said, 'This is no good, Susanna. *No good!*'" Susanna was glaring now at Melody, glaring. "So, see?"

"Well, was it?" said Melody calmly. "I mean, I don't know much about art, so maybe it wasn't any good, but you've got to do bad stuff sometimes, right? I mean, you should see the pies I make when I feel crummy, you can't even cut them, but I win lots of prizes, too. I do real good at the fair, better every year. So maybe it wasn't any good because you were feeling lousy when you did it. But maybe it even was, and she just didn't like it. You know, like one year the judges didn't like my chocolate-raspberry, the jerks, what did they know? I mean, who is this teacher, God? And this girl, Amanda, I don't know, but I'd say she just sounds jealous."

"Jealous?" echoed Susanna stupidly. "Uncle Louie, he said something about jealous. . . ."

"Sure," said Melody. "Because you can still do it and she can't. Well, you can't listen to people like that, Susanna, they'll drive you crazy. You don't want to end up like . . . sorry, okay, sorry, I always forget and say things I'm not supposed to. Besides, now that I've met the old guy I like him. Poor old guy, is he better this morning? Is he going to be okay?"

Jealous, God, crazy, and now Uncle Louie. Susanna couldn't help it, she started to laugh. She really couldn't help it, Melody was so funny, everything she'd been saying was so funny and she didn't seem to know it, and then Susanna was crying, she was so tired of crying, she never used to cry, and Melody was leaning over her and was patting her shoulder, and then the big wad of tissues Melody always carried for April was stuffed in Susanna's hand and she was mopping herself up.

"I guess you're saying he's not going to be okay," said Melody. "So . . . ?" She winced at herself. "Sorry," she said.

"It's all right," Susanna said, and sighed. "So he's gone. We took him to the hospital. They've got him now. He'll never come back."

Melody pursed her lips, thinking. "He got anything to come back for?"

Susanna sighed. Her nose was still leaking; she gave it another swipe.

"No," she said.

"Yeah," said Melody. "That sucks. My mom, she had lots to come back for, she didn't make it either."

"Melody," said Susanna. "That . . . I wish I knew how to say it. . . ."

Melody, one more time, could be counted on to say it for her. "That really sucks," she said, and Susanna nodded.

"Yeah," she said. "That really sucks. Melody, that picture? You know, the picture of your mom? I thought, well, I *do* still want to do art and I used to be good, and I know, anyway, that I can draw okay. Even when I was little, I could make people that looked like people. Well, I thought maybe I could draw a picture, your mom, you, April, all of you together. I've got pastels here, if you think it might be something you'd like to have."

Melody was silent for such a long time that Susanna finally had to look at her. Melody's hair was still too short, she still bulged, but her eyes no longer looked either shrewd or wary, and there wasn't anything bloblike about her at all. Her mouth was moving, but not, for once, with words, and then she dragged one last tissue out of the pocket of her jeans, used it, and cleared her throat.

"Yeah," she said. "That'd be something I'd like to have."

"Good," said Susanna. "Good." And it would be good. Because she probably wasn't really crazy, she could see that now. Or cursed. And if she wasn't, then she could work, work hard enough so it *would* be good. And when it was done she had something else to finish. It would be a painting, the hardest, most important painting she'd ever done. It would take her, probably, until she could come back here again, to Melody and April, to her grandfather, and to Uncle Louie, wherever he might be.

Her monkey tree. She could see it already in her head, the monkey tree she'd started so many days ago. It was crowded now, its branches sagging. But it was strong. And it was still growing, sending out new branches that would hold new monkeys, some of them big, some of them little, some of them young, some of them old, weak, slipping maybe, ready to fall. But none of them would really fall, be lost, be forgotten, because they'd all be hanging on. They'd all be hanging on to each other.

Practice, her father had said, and he was practicing now, somewhere above them, the scales moving to melodies, the melodies weaving faster, more and more complex, harder and harder, up and up, floating, sustaining, until it wasn't practice anymore, not practice at all. It was music.